THE
DEVIL
DRIVES

THE
DEVIL
DRIVES

by

Virgil Markham

RAMBLE HOUSE

ISBN 13: 978-1-60543-18-8

ISBN 10: 1-60543-018-8

Cover Art: Gavin L. O'Keefe
Preparation: Fender Tucker

THE
DEVIL
DRIVES

Oh, for the Life of a Warden!

AT ELEVEN O'CLOCK an agent from a mattress manufacturer came by appointment, and since the steward, as he was called, had mistaken the date and was not in the prison at the time, I took the agent on. When he had gone I was a long way behind my schedule, and it didn't cheer me to see my secretary, Randall, grinning at me when I reentered the office.

"Lady to see you, Warden. From—"

"No appointment, has she?"

"No, sir."

"Then I can't see her today, and you know it."

He still grinned. "Expect me to tell her that?" he said.

"Why shouldn't you tell her?"

"I'm leery, Warden. She's got something—"

"You must be off your feed. Tell her to make an appointment, tell her to come again, tell her not to come again—all the same to me. Did she give you a card?"

"I tried to tell you, she's from the Woman's Press Association. There on the blotter."

I read, "MISS LOUISA MATTHEWS CARMODY."

"Randall, you're fired," I said. "What the hell do you mean by almost letting this woman get away? Tell her to wait."

My secretary was still grinning all over his face while he marched out to Miss Carmody. I pulled out my latest correspondence file, and thumbed over the letters rapidly. Most of them had flimsy copies of my answers attached, but I hadn't answered this one, hadn't trusted myself to. I jerked it out.

My colleague over at Irving was the author. I can repeat his style though not his exact words:

DEAR WARDEN PETERS:

In case you should receive a visit from a Miss Louisa Matthews Carmody, representing the Woman's Press Association, I am writing you to let you know that this lady visited us without an appointment on a most inconvenient morning and requested to be allowed to inspect all parts of the prison and to have the opportunity to see each prisoner individually face to face, including those in solitary confinement. I felt it was impossible to accede to the request without investigating her credentials, especially as she either would or could not express any definite reason for her desire. Though all this was most unsatisfactory, as you will agree, when she again appeared at the prison, I permitted her, at her very urgent application, to see the men during exercise. As far as I know, there has been no aftermath of her visit, but on consideration I have come to the conclusion that it is not advisable to permit another such apparently meaningless inspection, and therefore I am writing to you.

Miss Carmody informed me that she had visited a great many of the principal penitentiaries of the East, and that she intended to visit as many more as possible, including Franklin. If she visits you, I should deem it not advisable to accede to her request. I am sure that you will receive this in the spirit in which it is given.

Fraternally,

I crumpled the sheet and chucked it in the waste-basket, and brought my fist down on the button that buzzed my secretary.

"The old codfish!" I thought. "That's what comes of having no brains and a Ph.D. Who does he think he is, my grandmother? Not advisable to accede! I'll give her a run for her money!"

She came in, and for an instant I had a strong desire to laugh. "Not advisable to accede." She was a small woman in a black cloth coat and black fur collar. She was carrying her hat in her hand and had thrown back the top of her coat.

I motioned her to a chair. "Madam, I have been looking forward to your appearance—ever since I was warned against you."

She sat perched on the edge of her chair, a trim little figure, perhaps inclining to be gracefully plump, with her smart shoes set close together and her soft little hands folded. Her face was rather plain but pleasant, with a touch of sallowness in her skin and long, dark brown hair containing streaks of gray, lying smoothly back from her forehead. Her features, not by any means as plump as her figure, and the way her head was set, or the way she carried it with her chin tilted, gave her an air of alertness, perhaps even of wariness. Her eyes as they took me in were pleasant and brown, and I noticed that even in her eyebrows there were traces of gray.

I wondered about her age. Her hair made me think forty at least. Then her eyes made me take it back.

She said, "Pardon me, you *are* the Warden, aren't you? I didn't expect—"

"No, Madam, you didn't," I said. "After Irving's warden you would hardly feature one like me."

"You are rather young, aren't you?" she asked, and then drew back in confusion. "I'm sorry."

"Not at all," I excused her. "They all think so, Madam, but you're the first one who's ever said it to my face. It wasn't my age, though, that you dropped in to see me about?"

"No, Mr. Warden." As she came to the point, I detected a slight movement of her features, a tightening, as if she was nerving herself for something. "I am, as you know, from the Woman's Press Association. I am making an investigation of prisons, and have visited several already and shall visit a good many more. I wish to—"

My face made her break off. "But you have heard of my visits, Mr. Warden?"

"Yes, Madam." I reached down and fished "not to accede" out of the waste-basket, smoothed it out, and handed it across to her. "In confidence, Madam," I warned, "you did not ring the bell with my brother in Irving."

"I see," she said. "Then do I understand, Mr. Warden, that you are opposed to me, too?"

"My brother in Irving is not my keeper, Madam. This prison is independent, and I am in complete charge here. At the same time, on the information I have there is nothing I can do for you. You wish to visit every part of the penitentiary and to see the men individually. Is that it?"

She nodded. "Exactly, Mr. Warden."

"For what reason, Madam?"

"Among other things I have in view, I have been commissioned to make a report to an anonymous party on men who are specially deserving of encouragement or in any way needing special help or, in case of their discharge, of financial assistance."

I told her bluntly that it sounded thin to me, and that I objected on principle to making a show of the men.

She stiffened up suddenly, and her hands became fists. "You may not understand, Mr. Peters, but you should understand this: I have been the means of helping quite a few in every place I have visited. Your friend at Irving does not mention it in his letter, but there are half a dozen prisoners there who deserve help and who will get it."

I paused a moment. "Well, Mr. Peters?" she said anxiously, and the calm, or pretended calm, of her earlier self was gone.

I still hadn't made up my mind, or perhaps I pretended to myself that I hadn't. I shook my head.

"Why not, why not?" she exclaimed. "It isn't irregular, is it, to show visitors about the prison and to allow them to see the men? Are you afraid that I am bringing in weapons or drugs?"

"If you are attempting to smuggle anything in here, you will not succeed."

"I see. Then why do you hesitate, Mr. Peters? If I am so harmless, that is."

I buzzed Randall. "I was thinking more of my morning's work," I said. "I will conduct you personally, Madam, over every portion of this prison, from the roofs to the basement."

"Oh, *thank* you, Warden Peters! But—you will let me see the men?"

"If you wish to see them as they file out from mess, you can."

Her eagerness would not be concealed. There was a flash of her even teeth and a glint in her eye, a look of gladness that was personal and intimate and had nothing to do, I was sure, with the Woman's Press Association.

"Randall," I said to my secretary, "I'm going to introduce this lady to Franklin; so take the rest of the day off and try to have a good time in this god-forsaken town. We'll work tonight instead of now. I'll talk to Dorsey and Edwards after mess. Let them have the regular grub."

I turned to my visitor. "This way, Madam," I said, and behind my back I tipped Randall a wink and made a sign with my thumb that said, "Somebody follow us up and keep us in sight."

We made the rounds of the cells and the mills and the chapel and the library and the yards and the wards and the keepers' lockers and the kitchen. I took her into the nearest thing we have to a dungeon, light and airy, with nice white tiles, but depressing just the same when you've been there solitary for a few days. A couple of big apes there made faces at us, and we passed on, but she had looked the inmates in the eye. I even took her into the death house because she asked for it.

"Did my friend at Irving let you do this?" I asked.

"No, but he—he let me see—their pictures."

Throughout the rounds she had seemed interested in everything, peering with her sharp little head, asking questions. I never had a more intelligent visitor, or one who understood more quickly the reason why we worked this or that in the way we did. Yet I felt that her primary interest was in the men themselves, not in the conditions.

I didn't change my mind when I observed her as the men came out of the mess hall in a double file. She tried to conceal the vital interest that she felt in them for some reason, but I don't think that one went by without her having a clear instantaneous photograph of him, his face, his hands, his walk. A number of times she turned to me quickly and indicated a man, and I made a mental note of him. Those she picked were in most cases such as I would have selected myself for consideration if I had been doing the humanitarian stunt.

We went back to the office, where I asked her if she would stay and eat a bite, as it was well past one. But she thanked me and said "No." I saw that she was disinclined to remain where she might have to answer questions instead of ask them. "If you will send the names of the men I chose to the Association, they will look into their cases. If you recommend others, they will be considered, too."

"With pleasure," I said. "When can I expect to read your account of the American penal system?"

"You had better not expect it before you see it, sir," she answered. She held out her hand. "Good-by, Mr. Warden. You've been more than kind. And I can't help saying that you really are young, sinfully young."

"Thank you, there's a reason."

"I wish I had the same reason," she said, and then an orderly, who had answered my buzz, escorted her to the gate.

I interviewed the trusties who had taken turns trailing me, and none had anything suspicious to report. "She carried her hat in her hand," was the most damaging thing either of them could say.

"She laid it down oncet," added the other. "In the ward."

"No one else went near it?"

"No, sir."

"Then there's nothing in the hat."

Randall's assistant, Peisner, came in to say that a call had come from the Lieutenant Governor. I was to escort a party of three through the cell-rows. Something to do with the Break-proof Prisons people.

"Oh, my God!" I exclaimed. I was fed up with prison.

"Yes, sir," said Peisner.

"Never mind 'yes, sir,' wise-guy. I'm going to lunch. No, I'll talk to those two tramps first. Have Edwards and Dorsey brought up."

While I ate my food I kept wondering about my woman visitor. I couldn't feel that her visit quite made sense, but I couldn't tell why. On the surface, perhaps, it had been a normal matter, but I couldn't slay the thought that there had been something about it I had missed. And about the little brown-gray woman herself there was something elusive and captivating. "My lady, you've not done with me yet," I said softly.

1

Frank Holborn Goes Out

MY NAME IS GEORGE LAWSON PETERS. A year ago I was Warden of Franklin Penitentiary, which is one of the two prisons in New Jersey where the death penalty is inflicted. I had held the job five years, and I was sick of it.

On October 17 we made preparations for electrocuting two gangsters. The first would be a Passaic killer called Porky Evarts. The other was a gunman with a long New York record, sentenced for murder from Franklin County. His name was Frank Holborn, and although I knew him better than most other men under my care, he was something of an enigma to me. He had glints of the gentleman everywhere about him, and he had been sentenced for one of the most atrocious killings I can remember.

Evarts would be taken to the chair at eight o'clock, and Holborn would follow immediately after the first execution.

That afternoon late, Peisner, one of the office men. complained of stomach trouble. He had been looking seedy all day. The prison is always stuffy, and it may seem more so than usual when a job like that night's is facing the community. It wasn't difficult to suppose that this young fellow, who had been with us only a couple of months, was getting nervy on the brink of his first execution. I had the doctor look at him and stick a thermometer into his mouth, and I tipped the doctor a wink to read the temperature a degree or two higher than it was. He did, and put young Peisner to bed in the special ward, since he had no chance of being looked after at the place he stayed in the town.

It was between twenty minutes and a quarter to eight when the State executioner reported that his apparatus was all fit and ready for action. A warder was waiting to enter the office just as the executioner went out. The warder said that Holborn wanted to speak to me. Within two minutes I was on my way to the death house.

From the death house there are two sets of doors, one inside the other, leading into the inner yard of the prison. Their keys hung in my office and were never removed except after an execution and the autopsy which follows, when the corpse was carried out through the doors. The dead-wagon, when it came, would enter at the rear and wait backed up part way into the inner court.

Just before I left the office to visit Holborn I glanced at the keyboard behind unbreakable glass, and noticed that the proper quota of keys hung from every peg.

I passed into the death house. The eight cells there are on either side of a little corridor of their own at right angles to the main passage, which leads straight on into the execution chamber. I could see through the open door where half of the ten witnesses were already standing against the further wall in there, silent as dummies.

I went to Holborn's cell. He was alone. He had refused religious consolation. Two cells away from him, Porky Evarts was talking to a priest. He had a high-pitched voice, and for the first minutes of my interview with Holborn I kept hearing the other man's words without getting their sense.

Holborn was a large man, and he had taken on weight in the death house. He attributed the fact to "insufficient exercise." He was, of course, in his death suit, with the slashes for the electrodes. He was about two-thirds through a big cigar. He wasn't puffing tensely or stolidly, but like any man who enjoys a cigar and knows how to get all the enjoyment there is out of it.

When he caught sight of me through the grill, he took the cigar out of his mouth, waved me a greeting with it, and smiled.

"Glad to see you, Warden. I wanted to have another of our little talks before eight o'clock. I don't know what my address will be after tonight."

He spoke deliberately. Then, as I didn't answer, his manner changed. His grin was broader than ever. "You know, Warden, you're too good-looking for a warden. You're too young to be locked up here. Educated, too—like me. Everything in your favor. You ought to get wise to yourself—grab off some racket—clean up." He chuckled. "Something of a roughneck too, eh? You fancy yourself as a bit of a tough. Maybe so. You'd be a killer with the molls too. You'd cut a wide swath. No kidding."

This wasn't new. Whenever I had spoken with Holborn at any length, he had dragged in this sort of persiflage. But I was surprised to have him greet me with it when the chair had been finally tested and was waiting for him.

"You're sick of it, aren't you? Rotten sick of it."

I just stood there glaring.

He went on, chewing the butt of his cigar vigorously as he spoke. "You ought to get out of this. It's going to tell on you, Warden. You're getting in a rut. Too bad."

"Was this all you wanted to say to me?" I asked harshly.

He laughed. "Not all," he said. "But I did want to get in one more little sermon—before—" He shrugged his shoulders. "Come in, Warden. I don't want to talk through a door."

I unlocked and entered the cell.

"That's better," said Holborn. I never saw a man more serious than he was then. He talked rapidly in a low tone. "I've been thinking this thing over a long time, but I've made up my mind and it won't take long to spill it. First, though, I'm going to tell you something that'll sound phony to you. This thing I'm taking the rap for—it's been framed. I can take it. Only don't forget—it's been framed. I want you to know that, Warden, because—well, because I'm human. I've been several kinds of a damn fool, but I'm no murderer."

I said, "I hope you're right."

"That's not so important. But this next is—for you. Maybe it'll sound like more old stuff, Warden. I want you to do something for me."

"Yes, I've done that a good many times. Anything I can do—"

He wouldn't let me pursue that line any further. His tone was businesslike; that's all I can call it. "I want you to promise." That made it out of the question for me to put up any conditions; I had to take it or leave it.

He kept pounding at me. "I want to show you I don't bear any grudge, Warden. I want to put you wise to something for your own good. You'll thank me, after. For your own good. I've been working on it—thinking it over—and it'll suit you down to the ground."

There had been hints of a similar nature in earlier talks he had had with me, but nothing as downright clear.

Barely ten minutes were left before I'd have to accompany Evarts to the chair. Just the same, I took time and considered. A few seconds more or less would make no difference to Evarts, or to the law. Should I give this man my promise, with the understanding that I'd undertake any amount of trouble if the matter was on the square?

"No," I said.

He didn't show surprise. He just nodded, and said, "Thanks, Warden." And then I began to tell him the why's and wherefore's. I got heated.

"All right, Warden," he grunted with a shrug. "Have it your own way. Let it go at that. No hard feelings."

Then I was aware that a guard was standing outside the cell; he had been knocking, and now he called, "Two minutes of, sir."

It was time to take Evarts to the chair.

"All right, Warden," said Holborn, while I left the cell. Then he added as an afterthought, a little louder, to make sure I'd hear, "Maybe there was a little revenge mixed up in it, but it wasn't anything wrong. Merely illegal. Maybe you'd never have found why I asked you." He was silent a moment, and then called after me, "You may be sorry you refused my legacy!"

The guards and I went to Evarts' cell and took him out. With hands grasping each of his elbows, preceded by the priest, he shambled round the corner of the little corridor and to the chair, still piping meaninglessly in that voice of his. Seven minutes later he was pronounced dead. He was the only man we executed that night.

Evarts' body was lugged over to a cot behind a screen to await an autopsy, and the guards went back for Holborn.

They brought him in. He still had the stump of his cigar between his lips. As he advanced step by step into the middle of the room, a look of bewilderment came into his face, as if it surprised him that the proceedings were going so far. Then he looked quickly about the room and stared at the spectators. He came to a halt, and the guards beside him, who held him by each arm, stopped, too. Instead of marching him straight to the chair, they seemed to take their cue from him.

At last his eyes met mine, and at what he saw in them he was plainly astonished. I spoke up. "Yes, Holborn, Peisner got the keys all right, but we didn't let him drop them through the infirmary window. Your friends who came in the dead-wagon to take you away alive are all covered by machine guns from the walls, and they know it. There won't be any break for your benefit tonight."

Something went down thud behind me. One of the witnesses had fainted.

Then I saw that Holborn had a gun in his hand. Where it came from I don't know. It was as inexplicable as one of Houdini's tricks, and a damned sight more dangerous.

I'm not one of the newer wardens. I kept a Colt strapped to my appendix whenever I went into the cell-rows. There are such things as hidden enmities and men blowing their tops all of a sudden in the best regulated prisons.

Holborn was jerking to one side, I believe to get behind one of the guards and use him for a shield, when I had my own gun out and shot him twice through the chest.

There was pistol-smoke still in the air when he lapsed into the coma he didn't come out of. Before that, I heard him through the smoke, "I don't blame you, Warden. I wouldn't have plugged you, though. You did your duty, damn your eyes. I hope you never have to buck a thing like this."

A minute later he whispered, "You may be up against it yet, promise or no promise." And a grin crossed his face, an ugly thing on the face of a half-dead man.

He died with some of that grin still registering.

2

The Pat to Dubrosky Letters

IT MIGHT HAVE BEEN a successful break at that, except for the fact that we knew all about it several days beforehand. Stoolies, of course.

The plan hinged on Peisner, who turned out to be a graduate of two of the best crook universities, Hell's Kitchen and Auburn. His part was to get the death house keys and drop them into the yard from a specified infirmary window. The morgue wagon would back its way into the yard, containing, instead of the usual attendants, five gunmen. In the darkness one of these would pick up the keys, a full quarter of an hour before eight o'clock.

The plotters had learned that Evarts would die first, and they intended to break into the death house between the executions, timing their move for ten past eight. They would unlock the doors from the outside, shoot their way in if necessary, and also shoot their way out—with Holborn.

When Peisner took the keys from the board, which I gave him plenty of opportunity to do unobserved, he substituted a set that resembled the originals. We allowed him to make this switch, allowed him to be by himself in the special ward, but just as he was going to drop the keys from a window, two husky guards discouraged him.

As for the gunmen, the moment the inner rear gate opened to admit the morgue wagon, a dozen guards, special deputies, and what not scrambled aboard and overpowered the occupants without firing a shot.

The attendants who belonged in the vehicle were picked up outside the city with a few bruises and a tale. They said that the wagon had been held up within two blocks of the undertaker's, and that they had been tied up and thrown out, with one of the gunmen standing guard over them in a lonely gravel pit until about half past eight. The authorities never learned who the higher-ups were.

I naturally played an important part in the inquiry, but my real interest in the whole affair centered on Holborn. I thought about those last hours of his, before he had made up his mind to send for me. What could it have been, so important, perhaps so risky or so much on the thin edge of the law, that he demanded my promise before he would tell me?

Finally I looked up the records on the crime for which he had been convicted. It was an open and shut case, the murder of a woman he had brought to Jersey and had been living with for some time. But he told me that he had been framed! In spite of my experience and common sense, that ridiculous statement, the declaration of every crook since the flood, somehow seemed to throw a shadow of doubt into my mind.

And then—while the uproar about the plot was tailing off and the gunmen were waiting to be sentenced—came the turning point. One afternoon I received an envelope which contained nothing but a number of old letters in longhand. The envelope was plain; there was no explanation. I glanced over the letters and I saw they had nothing to do with me.

My decision to take those letters home with me in the evening was the turning point of my career.

My rooms were just outside the prison, abutting on the wall. Technically, of course, I was living inside the prison, as required by law. After Mrs. Albert, my housekeeper, had given me my dinner, I went into the front room, referred to between us as my study, and sat down to examine the letters.

The envelope they had come in was postmarked City Hall Station, New York City. That was no help.

The letters inside, eight or ten in all, were fastened together with an elastic band and had been numbered with a blue pencil. This was decidedly helpful, for they weren't dated. The paper was a light pink shade, good quality, and the writing was large and sprawling thin, easy to read. I guessed at once, though the signature of all of them was "Pat," that a girl had been the writer.

There was no indication where they had been written or who the writer might be—except, of course that I might pick up something in the text of the letters themselves.

I read the first one, and a sort of spell took hold of me. I'll put the whole thing in here, for the letters are still available.

DEAR OLD DUBROSKY—I like your new name so let's forget all your many and various others, including your real one, for awhile. I never liked them as well for now I can picture you with a long curley beard which becomes you, and earings in your ears, and a big saber cut in your forehead, and a long cuttlas a your side and gallon boots and everything else that befits a pirate. It was such fun yesterday when you showed me where the doll's house would be, and even if I was late getting home and had to go to my room I had Browning's "Blot on the Scucheon" to read though mother doesn't know about it. Dear mother doesn't know about so many things. I suppose she wouldn't expect me to understand it anyhow, but I do of course. And even if I didn't have the "Blot on the Scucheon" I'd be glad for seeing you, because now you are my Dubrosky, and have earings, which are nice for a man to wear. I can think of you building the doll's house and be happy. It is frightfully odd, of course, for a pirate to be building one, but maybe you are a superanuated one or something, and maybe you are senile. But dear Dubrosky, I will never be able to think of you as old. When you came home you seemed just the same as when you were here first. I was only nine then, wasn't I, but I had good judgement.

Goodbye now, I hear mother's heavy tread on the stairs. I wish she had more modern ideas, but if she will cling to her outmoded generation I refuse to be intimadated by her.

PAT

How old was she? I pictured her, a little girl in a short skirt and a tam-o'-shanter, going hand in hand with her bearded Dubrosky—or was that beard imaginary, as the "earings" must be? Who was she? Where had these meetings been?

I read the next and the next. They were usually written soon after some encounter or walk or ride (there were references to horseback riding, once "along the shore") or skating party or exploring expedition. This was made "among the strange and storied shapes and the Malebolgian cliffs and icy wilderness of the shore. Indeed, Dubrosky, they are most terrifyingly Malebolgian." What could this mean? Even when I had checked "Malebolge" I wondered where in the U.S.A. such cliffs could be.[1]

Most of the letters had been done while the girl was still feeling the thrill of the man's presence, this man evidently old enough to be her father. Their meetings had to be secret, for "It wouldn't do for us to be seen together. People would talk if they knew, especially the Maitlands and the Rapagos. You know what *they* are!"

The concluding letter ended:

I think it is safe to leave the letters where we always have been doing. Albert Jones comes by the orchard sometimes, and I met him there once with his dog, but he cannot suspect anything. And I know that mother doesn't suspect anything because she is the worst actress imaginable, and if she did she couldn't keep it secret for one minute. Isn't it silly that I can't allow her to know? Next week I shall get. away from Padgett's early and meet you before going home.

So the series closed and I felt a peculiar disappointment that the story went no further. It was exasperating to have so little to go on, so much unsaid. But what was there raised pictures in my mind as vivid as anything I had ever read in books. For me the charm of the girl Pat was a true and lasting thing, and perhaps the circumstances in which I was reading the letters added to the atmosphere they produced. How had I come to get them? What was I to do with them? There was nothing I could do, except destroy them, and I was unwilling to do that. Instead, in the course of the week, I read them two or three times.

Then days later I received another envelope just like the first, containing about fifteen more letters. That day I let myself out of jail early, went home, read the batch right away.

And again afterward. The more I read, the more I got wrapped up in the story. The first letter had been written just a day or two after the last of the other lot, and it contained:

DEAR DUBROSKY—*When* are you going to let me see the doll's house? I do believe you intend to keep me waiting

---

[1] Mr. Peters might have explained: Malebolge is the eighth circle in Dante's "Inferno." The name means "the evil trenches."

until I'm too old to enjoy it. At my age, I've heard mother say, my tastes may be expected to change very rapidly. But, dear Dubrosky, I'm sure that there are two things my taste will never change for: for plays and for you. The only trouble is that we are three hundred miles away from any plays that are worth seeing. So I have to fall back on you. You had better look out, though, if you expect to make me believe that a doll's house that you have bean building all winter will take you all summer, too. I can be very fierce, you know, and my fierceness will strike those I like most hardest. . . .

Then:

Oh, Dubrosky, it is the loveliest doll's house—and of course you were right not to show it to me until you had the dolls. Dolls, and such dolls! After reading the "Blot on the Scucheon" I had serious doubts that I would ever be able to get interested in my dolls again. But I never saw such dolls as yours. And the house, two stories—and such a *divine* little attic. Of course you have to stand quite a way away to be able to see it all, but it is glorious and it *has* been worth all the work you must have put in on it. It was wonderful enough to see it standing there, but when you opened it up and showed me the pigmy tribe inside, then indeed I did think you are the most wonderful Dubrosky in the world, in the whole wide world.

I hear mother's approach. I must hide this, but I'll get it "posted" tonight just the same.

Half a dozen letters described more meetings and happiness together, sometimes at the doll's house, which Pat almost always described as "lovely," "wonderful," and "divine."

There was a new turn in the story:

Dubrosky, Dubrosky, what will happen to me now? Shall I pine on bread and water for the rest of my days? How disgusting it was for us to meet mother face to face, and very much face to face, after I had so cleverly had that headache at Charters' and had to come home. I wish I had come home. I think it's all so miserably silly, don't you? When we aren't doing anything wrong to see each other just because we happen to like each other. Of all the insane reasons for forbidding me to see you, because you have a bad reputation and are a man, while I'm only a little girl. Oh, yes, I've known that about you all along. But you've always been so beautiful to me. What on earth do they imagine you'd do to me? Ruin me? Murder me? Eat me? Of course, at my age, mother thinks I am just a silly infant who wants to do things because I've been told not to. But in reality in some ways I am more mature than she is—yes, you know I am, and I shouldn't wonder if she does too. Maybe that makes her more scared about me.

Now I've been locked in here almost two days, and nothing to do but read and nothing but last year's magazines to read. It would be so good, Dubrosky, if you would send me something to read instead of these. A nice long letter, or a poem, if it's not too much trouble.

Oh, Dubrosky, why shouldn't I admit I love you? Mother has just been in here and accused me of it. She has now had two tantrums in my presence, and I am beginning to enjoy them. Isn't thirteen old enough to know your mind? Juliet was only fourteen, Professor Gosling said. I don't care if she has found out. I don't care what she chooses to think or what she imagines that is so much worse than the dear truth about you Dubrosky. I don't care what she tries to do. YOU aren't afraid of her, are you, Dubrosky? Well, I'm not, and I shall tell her so the next time she tries to intimadate me. Oh, dear, if I only weren't so young in years!

I shall have to be very careful getting out of the window to post this tonight. Please answer quickly.

I've been reading more old magazines, but I won't read any more of that horrid one that's making Mr. Postum so much trouble. As if the people who sell patent medicines and things like that aren't doing a good to humanity.

I think I hear a third tantrum approaching—so goodbye. I'll mail this if it kills me.

Jailed PAT.

Pat was still a prisoner when she wrote:

Dubrosky, mother is simply too bad for anything. Imagine her, trying to tell me that during your wanderings abroad you haven't been away at all, but in jail!

Poor mother! I know now what subterfuges she is capable of descending to.

And yet, you know, Dubrosky, you really *are* a very wicked person. According to strict people like grandmama, you are quite horribly depraved. Her religion—or maybe religions—would just shriek at you. Tell me why this is, when I know that you are the nicest person in the world. You might make a poem of it, if it isn't too much trouble.

Jailed PAT.

The poem was delivered as ordered, and the next letter burst out in a torrent of praise:

Oh, your poem, Dubrosky, your wonderful, funderful poem! I would like to wear it next to my heart, but with mother in the vecinity it's too dangerous. I must hide it very secretly. I have copied it in my own hand, and then if she finds it I can just say languidly that it's something I did myself. That's why I am returning your own copy—I wouldn't destroy it for anything. You won't mind, will you, if I call it a creation of my own, in an emergency? I do adore it most profanely, from

> An object more completely ramshackle
> Than Bethel's former princely tabernacle

> to

> And hence no one with common sense
> Will venerate the commandments.

But in a way it's such an improper poem that mother may be more dire if I say I wrote it than if she knows I received it from you.

If Grandmama saw it! The roof would fly.

Then—last letter of the series—a tragic contrast:

Dubrosky, you traitor and coward, you, and so *mean!* Yes, mean, small, low! Oh, going in an hour, and I haven't even time to write all that my *anger* dictates. How can you? Is it mother who's made you do this? Are you ever going to write to me from your travels? Are you even going to remember me? Judging from what I have overheard mother say about your past life, I should think you won't. But you will, you will, you will!! And sometime let me hear from you, no matter how short your letter is. I really couldn't bear not to hear from you once in a long, long while.

Your abandoned PAT.

Might that be the end of the whole story? I waited a week, two weeks, before another envelope came. It contained only one letter and a fragment of two others. In addition, a card fell out of the envelope, a plain card with these words printed on it in pen and ink:

"I KNOW YOU'RE READING THEM WARDEN—KEEP IT UP. YOU KNOW ME."

These letters were of a different time and type. The paper was white, the writing less straggling and childish, the margin straight, and the spelling better. As I judged from the internal evidence, at least two years must have gone by since the earlier writing.

The first fragment had this to say:

. . . such fun since you came back, and now it seems as if you had never been away. To reopen the doll's house and find that no one had broken in and spoiled it, to go on the same walks and explorations together, and to know that we are just as we were before. We are both very young, Dubrosky, and the years will never change either of us, only you were older before you stopped growing older, that's all. Yes, you are the same old pirate who took me along the shore and into Murder Cove and rescued me so many times, and pirate you will be forever and a day. Thank the gods that mother is still in New York and hasn't appeared upon the scene as yet. It will be hard living with her when she learns that you have come back. Poor dear, what a difficult existence for her, just having to be herself. I pity her. But if she . . .

The second fragment:

. . . true to piracy still. What fun it was to hide our treasure, or rather the treasure that *you* supplied from the scrapings of all the bureaus (or should it be bureaux) you have encountered abroad. Some of the old dirty glass jewelry looked *so* realistic! And those big black pennys might have been dubloons, they were so disguised. It was very clever of you to think of the place, too, sealed so that no one will ever find it, except by earth, air, and water. I'm sure that until the end of the world no one will ever find it. But my Dubrosky is clever, and he is as good as he is clever. Do you know, I wish sometimes that you weren't quite so good as you try to be with me. That night in the moonlight, when the fog came so suddenly and you almost lost me. I never had realized that the cliffs were so steep. You helped me down so gallantly, and then—well, you washed your hands of me. I know that if I had been some other woman, you wouldn't have been so insultingly polite. And tomorrow mother arrives, and what will happen then is beyond my imagination . . .

And last, at the very last, the complete letter:

Dear, dear Dubrosky—please forgive me if I do not write very well. I have been crying just a little. I know I'm silly. But now to have you going around the world again, when you have been here such a little while, and I have to stay here and have nothing to remember you by except the doll's house and visiting where our treasure is hid, which I will guard faithfully and never disturb. Dear, dear Dubrosky, what shall I do? If only you would take me with you. I'm not too young, as you keep saying. But you are going alone, and your earrings will shine in other lands and foreign ladies will toy with them and you will while the days away with love all day long. I should think you would get sick of it, but of course I can't say from experience.

Anyhow, you broke it to me nicely, though it's a wonder that I didn't fall down on the ice, since my skating isn't what it was two years ago. It was nice of you to stay with me all afternoon, our last afternoon together. For that is what it will be.

I am not going to prolong this. I can't say any more, except that I am still your little girl, and always will be.

I suppose mother is at the bottom of it all again.

Your Pat.

I had thought that this was all, but inside the folded letter was a frantic final note that swung the story in a new direction, and left it hanging in space!

Oh, I can't stand it! She has driven me. What is she, to tell me what I should do, when she's been carrying on with that ghastly Prince person for six months. I hate her!

I'm coming with you, Dubrosky. You can't keep me from coming. She's slandered you to me for the last time. She'll never have another chance.

Dubrosky, you may dodge and you may twist, but I will join you either in New York or on the Continent. You have told me too much about your plans to get away from me. And we will be happy. I know we will.

I am so happy now that I can hardly hide it from *her!*

Au revoir!

Your everlasting PAT.

That was the end.

Suddenly it came over me what all this meant. These letters were being fed to me, fed to me slowly so that I would catch fire more surely. I had guessed that, but I knew something else now. This was the entering wedge of the proposal Frank Holborn had wanted to make to me.

At first there might seem to be a withering incongruity between these letters and Holborn, convicted murderer in Franklin prison. But really there was not. He, just like me, had been able to feel the tug of the story of the girl Pat and her lover Dubrosky. The reason they had been sent to me in spite of my refusal to make a promise, was that he had set some mechanism in motion before that night and he had not been able to cancel the arrangement. I still had to make the choice that had been given me in his cell.

What choice? I wondered, overtime. Would there be more letters?

No, but an envelope came the week after the series had ended. Inside was another plain card with a short printed message:

"WILL CALL FOR YOU AT 7:30 THURSDAY, BRING THE LETTERS. YOU KNOW ME."

At 7:30 Thursday a large limousine of some dark color drew up in front of the house. It was empty except for the chauffeur.

3

"Live Gloriously . . . and Highly"

I LAY BACK in the cushions and watched the lights fly by, and thought. We moved fast. Perth Amboy, Railway, Elizabeth—was it New York we were headed for? No, we turned more west, finally snaking through Passaic and the rest of the way through the frosted winter countryside.

I couldn't help wondering what the idea behind the whole thing was and what was going to come of it all. It was a grope, sheer guesswork, of course. I hadn't even a hint of what lay beyond the greedy headlights of the Packard, the strange road I was to travel, one vivid adventure telescoped into the next, at the end a nine days' wonder that had the whole East guessing, a thing too incredible to be humanly true—and the clue in my hands all the while. Then—a lightning-stroke. A road there's no retracing.

We turned in at a gate with a lodge alongside of it and drove half a mile, mostly among thick trees. Then we were in the open again and stopped at the foot of a flight of broad stone steps. The driver opened the door of the car and I got out and walked up the steps. I had just a glimpse of a terraced garden below me in the moonlight, and the impression of some kind of Italian architecture about the house, which was on a palatial scale, when the front doors opened wide and a butler and footman stood waiting to receive me in the vestibule.

I walked in without a word. The butler closed the door and the footman took my hat and eased my light overcoat off me.

"Not with this gentleman!" said the butler sharply, and I was just in time to see the footman draw his hands back from beside me. Sure as Christmas, he had been going to frisk me! I had a gun, too.

The butler said, "Yes, sir, this way, sir," as if I had made some remark, and we set out down the hall. There was nothing phony about the butler, as far as I could see. He was a real butler, and they are certainly a class of men apart.

I followed him a furlong, it seemed, down hallways lined with paintings and statuary that looked good to me. He bowed me into a little room done in light oak paneling and left me there with "If you will wait here, sir. Please help yourself to cigars."

It was all right with me. I sank deep into an armchair and waited for whatever might happen.

The next moment a man in dinner dress was standing there. He was somewhere in his early forties, a chap with a big, ruddy face, not such a bad face as the faces go I was used to, clean shaven, with heavy black brows and rounded jowls. He had a handsome smile.

I recognized him well enough! Why, we had once been kids together at school. Before old man Aldrich got too rich. Sam Aldrich, which is close enough for a name, was the son of a Solicitor General long dead. He himself had run for Lieutenant Governor on a ticket that was barely defeated. He was one of the wealthiest men in the state, and though no one knew exactly how he got his money, nobody doubted that he was a genteel racketeer, in fact, probably the biggest shot in New Jersey. He certainly had bootleg affiliations.

"Shake, Warden," he said. He sat down opposite me and drew his chair close to me. "Let's get to work. Do you know where you are and who I am?"

"Sure. I remember the Taylor Street school, and—"

"Well, we'll mention no names," he said with a smile that drew his mouth up at one end and down at the other. "And you'd better forget what you *think* you know. It will be impossible, of course, for you to prove that you have been here tonight."

"I suppose it will be," I agreed.

"Good man. You've got those letters with you?"

"I have. But weren't you risking—?"

"Oh, they've been photographed. Let's have them."

I pulled them out of my pocket, and he took them, glanced over the numbers. "You've read them all, of course?"

"I have."

"Interested in them?"

"I was interested, yes."

"Damn right you were!" He pulled his heavy brows together a moment, and when he spoke it was like a gat spitting out slugs. "I'll tell you what those letters are.

Warden. They're my bait. I guessed the letters would hook you. I figured right, didn't I?"

"So far," I admitted.

"Then you're the man I want!" he said. "The fact that you came here proves it. Holborn knew!"

"I said 'So far,' " I reminded him.

"You're going further," he told me decisively, and his business-like statement was more impressive than any gangster's growl could have been.

"Maybe," I grudged.

My host grunted. "Here's your history, and how I have you lined up. You had a fair high school education in Camden, and then you tried Rutgers for a while. Finally your father told you to cut the comedy and get to work. He got you a tin badge and a job as a detective in Trenton."

He looked at me humorously. "Want me to tell you how good you were?"

"Sure, go ahead. Nobody ever did before."

"That's right. You were a good detective, Warden. You liked the story-book angle of it, and you could stick to the routine too. But you resigned?"

"I did."

"And I know why. Surprises you, don't it? You did the work and others got the credit. Two big cases, and you got the freezeout when the promotions came. You were too young. Right?"

"Damn right."

"You see I know. You were good, all right. . . . Well, as I was saying, you quit. But you'd learned some politics. Two years later and you were in so good with Tim Snead and his crowd that they gave you a step up by creating an assistant wardenship at Franklin and sticking you in. Then Brady died and you were right in line for his position. It was a public scandal making you a warden so young."

"Why not?" I countered. "In Chicago they have a university president that's just been weaned, haven't they?"

He waved his cigar. "Sure, sure. I've got no kick. Why not? But you've been at Franklin—let's see—going on your fifth year, aren't you? You're still a kid. Furthermore you're not married. What about it? Have I the dope?"

"I can't improve on it," I admitted.

"There's more. Warden, you're sick of your job. You want air. You want to wave your arms and legs and get up some mornings at three p.m. You're getting so that chair in the office gives you a pain. You want to get out of jail. You don't look, talk, or act like a warden. In fact, you're a man of the world. Well, why shouldn't you be?"

I made a struggle to speak, but for the moment I was tongue-tied—and sick. He had hit the nail on the head, all right. That feeling that I was in a box had been growing on me for a long time. Now to have this man tell me what I was thinking shook me.

"What's all this about?" I exploded suddenly. "What the hell are you driving at? Are you trying to hook me into some deal? I'm not available if you expect me to do any dirty work. I may be losing interest in my job, but I'm not ready to turn crooked."

He held up his hand again. "Let me do the talking now. You later. What I want you to do is to take Frank Holborn's job."

I stared at him. Maybe my mouth was open, or I looked foolish enough without it, for he laughed out loud. Then he was plenty serious, and leaned over and tapped my sleeve.

"Holborn was a criminal. Is that it? Well, yes, he was, but he had a start something like you, Warden. Good family, education pretty good, interested in more than money. I wasn't using him for anything actually fishy, something else altogether, when he ran into this rap. Do you believe me?"

"What of it?"

"The job he was doing for me—I wouldn't have handed it to any flashy crook, who'd have curled up in the death house. If you take it, Warden, you may have to play the gentleman. Think you can? I think so. The real question is, can you impersonate a roughneck too?"

"I haven't asked for it yet."

"I know that. I know that. But if you can, I'll make you a sporting offer."

"What's a sporting offer mean to you?"

He laughed. "O.K. I'm going to spill everything to you, and maybe you'll change your song some. Reading those letters, did you sometimes wonder what the other gink wrote back to this girl Pat?"

Of course I had.

Aldrich reached into his inside pocket and brought out two envelopes clipped together. He separated them, laid the big one on the table, and gave the other one to me.

"Read that."

I looked at the outside of it first. It was, a cheap paper, and it was now very dirty. The stamp was foreign and I couldn't recognize it. The postmark meant nothing to me. The writing was dark and close and spiny, all on one side with an exaggerated slant, very hasty-looking and irregular. The address was

Miss Philadelphia Boston,
    Care of The Archery Company, Ltd.,
        Billitston-by-Cripplegate,
            London, E. C.
                England.

The handwriting of the letter inside was even more ir-regular, and I guessed that the writer had been a sick man when he wrote it. It straggled and made sags across the page, and it was sometimes feeble, sometimes stronger. This is what I read:

"Eleventh of May
Dearest and most adorable princess:

I've come to the last port of all. Your Dubrosky is dying in a dirty little town whose name fits his. Cholera, more or less. It's hard going, princess, and harder because I haven't seen you for three years and looked forward so to . . . my fault, of course, since you have been in England so long . . . and I never came. You are a woman grown now, and queenly, and it's my cursed luck to lose you, when you're worth ten thousand times any of the women I've gone to hell with. My cursed luck, also well deserved.

But there's something else I want you to know. You have my love and my soul and my all. I want you to have my all. In case anything should happen to the nostrum business . . . a time may come when universal Health will banish dosing . . . But in any case it was all intended for you. May your life be freer and richer because of it. Bless you, princess . . .

I almost forgot to tell you what it is. You remember the buried treasure that we put where no one would ever find it except by wind, earth, and water? Grand concealment, safe for centuries? That's it. You didn't know it, dearest, but it was real treasure I buried there . . . my all. It wasn't

pretended . . . it was real. You will find pearls and dia-
monds there. Enough to keep you the rest of your life . . .
enough to keep ten . . . and recover it and keep it and use
it. Be a real princess. I want you to live gloriously . . . I'll
write that again—gloriously . . . and highly. But give a
thought sometimes to Dubrosky in his personal private
hell . . . happy for you.

I know you're going back to America soon, but the
Archery people will redirect this if it doesn't find you there.
So, your Royal Highness, your humble Dubrosky bids you
farewell.

For the last time,
Goodbye, princess,
DUBROSKY.

I laid the paper down. I noticed that my hand trembled a
little. I gave a low whistle and found myself shaking my
head.

Aldrich was grinning at me. "I see it gets you, Warden.
Now can you guess what the job is?"

"I can see what—it might be."

"That's what it is."

"Do you mean to tell me—" I lifted the sheet and shook it
"—that you don't know—?"

"We don't know who wrote those letters, Warden. That's
the first thing to find out."

"Oh. And after that—you mean you want to recover the
treasure?"

"Damn bad."

I burst into a laugh. "But you're crazy. Don't you
see?—she's taken it away—"

4

Soapy Becomes Useful

"No , SHE NEVER took it away," he countered. "Not this Pat. And judging from this wind, earth, and water stuff, it's a million to one that nobody else did either."

"How do you figure—"

"Easy to guess, Warden, but I'll tell you. She never opened the letter."

"What! Never—"

"I opened it myself for the first time," he grinned, "back in the spring."

"Good God! Have you figured out when it was written?"

"Seventeen years ago."

"That's a long time for a letter to go unopened. Why didn't she open it? She couldn't have lost interest, do you think?"

"Did she ever get it?" he came back. "Was she alive to get it? It wasn't called for, and this place in London where he sent the letter probably had no address for forwarding anything sent to such a fake name as that."

" 'Miss Philadelphia Boston'?" I quoted. "Sounds like a beauty contest. Only a dame can't represent two cities."

"I don't know, don't care. Somehow it got together with the others, unopened, and, as I said, we—came across them."

He leaned forward suddenly and put his hand on my knee. His fingers clamped down. "Take it up where Holborn left off. Find who these people were. Find the real name behind the phony Philadelphia Boston. Get your hands on that treasure. You'll get a good split. Fifty percent of it's yours. You can probably retire then and try art or something."

"I'll have to consider—" I said it slowly, but I felt the impulse inside me gathering speed, getting dangerous.

"Consider be damned! What have you got to consider? Your wife and children?"

"No-no, but—" I was thinking fast, but I don't know what I thought. I can't tell all that was in my mind that made me do what I did next. A chance for release from the rut, a touch of glamour in those letters, a wish to find what Frank Holborn was going after, a little of the heavy influence of

Sam Aldrich, and an eagerness to do the thing for the pure hell of it as well as the money—I don't know. Anyhow, I saw opportunity grinning at me, and I grinned back. I said, "I'll take it."

"Good! You've got horse-sense, Warden. It's a record. Most men would have taken a week." He pushed me the big envelope on the table. "Instructions in there. Tells you all that Holborn had doped out. You can stand on his shoulders."

Yes, I got a thrill when I picked up that envelope. I was to carry on the work of my friend the murderer, that I had shot! "A drink?" said Aldrich.

"Yes, I'd like a drink now." He poured whiskies. "And one other thing you haven't told me. How did you get this material?"

He didn't respond at once, just tasted his drink. "Well, why not?" he said finally. "Starts you from scratch. I'll see if the man himself isn't in the garage." Behind a panel was a house telephone. He pressed a button and asked for a name. Then, "Have him come over. Yes, I want to see him," and to me, "A couple of the boys always sleep on the place. It's safer."

"Sure." I debated with myself whether to ask the next question. "You know, Ald—that is, I'm surprised you're so sentimental about this thing. Why all this fuss—spending money—all this—?"

"No, I'm not sentimental." He snorted at the word. He looked at the floor, his mouth forming shapes. "Dubrosky and the girl can be damned for all I care. But the competition is heavy—and so is the overhead. . . . Besides, there are others who'd look well in real jewels."

A moment later the butler, showing distaste, ushered in a hairy-fisted bruiser in corduroys and a leather jacket, who looked at his boss inquiringly.

"About getting those letters," said Aldrich. "Spill it."

"Sure." Then commenced a short pithy tale. The bruiser had been to a Manhattan warehouse getting some—

"Drygoods," inserted Aldrich neatly.

"Sure, drygoods." He was crossing town before running up to the Fort Lee Ferry when there were shots inside a house he was approaching. That alone wouldn't have made him stop, but up on the fire-escape he saw a man's figure beside a second floor window. The man must have been trying to get away, but he was caught somehow on the shutter pin. At that moment some drunken motorist passing in a small car rubbed up against the truck, breaking glass and not stopping. The bruiser jumped down to make a quick inspection. Finding that the small car had suffered all the damage, he was about to hurry from there when he noticed a man's figure making speed away up the block. The funny part was that the fellow had on only half a coat, the rest evidently being left on the fire-escape.

Furthermore, in the middle of the sidewalk a bunch of letters was lying. Some had become separated from the rest and were blowing about. The truckman scooped up those he didn't have to chase, and made off.

"Weren't the letters in anything?"

They had been in a fat envelope that had broken open. The driver had picked that up too, but couldn't find it later. He had seen the address, though.

"You did!"

Sure. It was addressed to the District Attorney or something.

"Good Lord! And this shooting—ever hear anything more about it?"

Clubfoot Jake Sabati had got it. They said that some dope had put slugs in him. The dope was never taken up.

"The killing and the letters—any connection?"

Aldrich said, "None whatever. The killing was strictly wop. Holborn found that much."

That being all he had to tell, the driver accepted a drink and departed.

"Well, what do you think of it?" asked Aldrich. "Good enough?"

"What about money?"

"Plenty, in reason. Two hundred in here." He flicked the envelope. "A thousand on deposit in the Pennsy Trust Company's central office. Name of John Williamson and a signature on record that a kid could imitate. The sample signature's in here too. If you need more, put an ad in the paper saying that the rent has been raised and your initials, J.W. I take the Times. But don't come around here till you have the goods."

He pushed the button alongside the door. "Oh, by the way, Warden, how are you going to get out of jail? What's your excuse for resigning?"

"I don't think I'm going to resign. I'm going to be fired. Or I'll resign under fire."

He scowled. "Oh, yes? What's the idea?"

"I want my picture to be in every paper in the East. I want every crook to get an eyeful of it. Then I won't be recognized when I work a disguise."

He laughed. "That's clever. Damn good psychology, too. Your mind *does* work, doesn't it?"

The footman had answered the bell, and he helped me into my coat and showed me out.

Next day I proved that I could be a very realistic warden of the old school.

There was a confirmed sogerer, malingerer and general troublemaker in the prison that we had hardly ever been able to get anything on.

I had him sent into the office next morning and told the clerk to leave us alone.

"Soapy," I said, "I've just heard that you were at the bottom of that trouble in the mill last week. Did you plant that file on Svendson afterwards?"

His eyes popped out with fright, and his mouth was wide open. He wheezed, "I don't know nothing about it. Honest to—"

I hit him on the point, and hurt him a little. I called in a guard and had him carried out.

I waited a couple of days, hoping that nature would take its course without any more assistance from me. It did. Word got out that a convict was near death as a result of months of brutal treatment at my hands. A friend of the other candidate for warden when old Brady died wrote a letter to the editor of the *Express,* and the paper took up the cudgels.

The rest was easy. In less than two weeks an investigation got under way, and it was surprising how many convicts there were who could remember a long course of cruelty at my hands beginning years back. Soapy was a star, and I admired his imagination, which even the testimony of the doctors couldn't kill.

When the going got where I estimated it couldn't get any hotter, I submitted my resignation, which was accepted. Later on I sent Soapy chocolates and tobacco, enough to last until his parole if he had good behavior. He got a pardon a month later!

5

The Settlement on Avenue A

IN THE Middle West I began my campaign with a transformation.

I fixed myself to escape recognition, in a cheap hotel room in Pittsburgh, while waiting for my return train. At a shabby barbershop there I first got a "tough" haircut, square across the back and close on the sides, giving a raw appearance at the edges. Then in my room I shaved off my mustache and cut away my eyebrows across the top of my nose where they almost met. I slipped a gold tooth, procured while I was still at Franklin, into place at the corner of my mouth.

Looking in the mirror when the operation was complete, I hardly recognized myself. I didn't even look like my cousin. If I had gone back to Franklin and told them I was the ex-warden, they would have locked me up.

Thus in a new guise I reached Hoboken on one of those slow and early trains that disgorge all-night day-coach passengers long before breakfast time. Then came the ferry ride through the morning mist, and West Street.

I looked out over the Hudson for some sign of the incoming night boat from Albany which would dock soon at the next pier and realized that I was hungry. The blurred yellow light of the coffee-shop that had just opened on the other side of the pier-entrance looked most inviting. I visited it.

The minutes dragged into quarters of an hour, and the street along the water-front had become a roaring crush of traffic when the boat hove in sight. I decided to wait and watch.

I looked on for a little while, but among the crowd was only one person who caught my interest, and that because, if my guess was right, he was an incongruous item in that throng of winter travelers and joy-makers. A slight, wizened man in a suit of loud check pattern, jeweled pin in his tie, and patent-leather shoes, he bore all over the marks of a cheap little yegg who had become temporarily flush. I noticed that instead of trying to claim a taxi, he was looking about him with uncertainty. Once he seemed about to compete for a cab, then changed his mind, and commenced gazing up and down the street again. Then I lost sight of him, and I wondered how far off my rather fantastic idea of him was.

I myself waited a number of minutes to avoid the worst of the rush, then singled out a car in the waiting line. I was about to give the address of a cheap hotel just above Greenwich Village when I caught sight of my little yegg again. A large—no, huge, enormous—yellow town car had stopped a little way up the street. In itself it was enough to draw the attention of anyone, but for me there was an additional flash of memory. I recalled a vague reference in one of Holborn's memos attached to the Pat-Dubrosky letters—a reference to somebody whom he called "a yellow big shot with a big yellow car." Certainly this chap I had observed could be nobody's "big shot," but the car did fit the phrase that had registered with me.

What was my surprise and consternation to see the patent-leathers and the check suit hurrying toward it! The little yegg—that title fits him as well as anything else—not merely climbed but actually dived into the darkness of the machine.

The driver of my cab evidently mistook my abstraction for loss of memory, but I took him by the arm and steered his sight toward the yellow car. "Follow that," I said, and slipped inside the taxi. A grand way to enter Manhattan without calling attention to myself! The driver slammed down the meter flag with the inevitable "O.K.," and the game of follow-the-leader was on.

I cursed myself several times during the next half hour, while we jounced and slithered over the pavements of downtown Manhattan. But I still believed that the little check-suited man was a yegg of some sort. I was sure that the big yellow omnibus was not his, and that he had flung himself into it because someone else was inside and that someone was impatient. Some dim guess of the possible usefulness of my pursuit was in the back of my mind.

For a half an hour my driver kept up a discreet pursuit while the Juggernaut maintained a zig-zag route generally from west to east. At length, when I was least expecting it, at a traffic stop 'way over east in the neighborhood of Grand Street, the little yegg slipped out as quickly as he had got in and was sauntering along on the sidewalk, apparently no more interested in the big yellow car than the next man.

That in itself seemed to prove that there was something wrong with the line-up, and I stuck to my determination to see the thing through.

My driver was asking through the space left by the sliding glass, "Wichdja want me to follow?"

"The little guy."

Two blocks further, my eye having left him for a moment, the little yegg had dropped out of sight. "Where is he?" I called.

The driver swung round the corner, and I was just in time to see the entrance door of the lofty brick building alongside us swinging shut.

Just then a mob of kids burst out of the building by a door further along Avenue A. I realized that it was Saturday morning, so this wasn't a school. The place must be some sort of a Settlement House.

"Hold it a minute," I told the driver and passed in the yegg's door. I found a small, plain lobby, with a desk at one side and elevator shafts facing the entrance. Above the desk an extensive file of letterboxes verified my guess that this place took lodgers.

I took off my hat and spoke to the girl behind the desk. She was rather more than a girl, a spinster with severe turned-down mouth-corners. My haircut didn't impress her favorably.

"You understand, of course, that our rooms are principally for young people engaged in art or professional work," she remarked forbiddingly.

"Well, I'm young people, I guess," I grinned.

"You may enroll tentatively if you wish," she said frigidly. "Your references—"

"Oh, my references will be all right," I said. "Mr. and Mrs. Bolster of Canton, Ohio, stayed here four or five years ago."

"I don't recall the name."

"That was quite some time ago."

"Yes, it must have been before we had the new building."

"It was, all right," I agreed.

Well, a minute or two later I was paying off my cab. I had signed my name in the register as John Williamson, the signature Aldrich had given me to use with my account at the Pennsylvania Trust, and I decided to give the Trust

Company as a reference. This name and that of "Terry Fultz" were all that I intended to adopt.

My eye happened to be on the elevator indicator, and I saw that the car was starting down from the fourteenth floor. Seventeen was the top. The pointer swerved without a stop, until it touched the level, the door opened, and out walked the little yegg alone.

I asked the elderly girl at the desk if she couldn't fix me with a room about on the fourteenth or fifteenth floor. By luck, one of the vacant rooms was on the fifteenth, and so it was I came to be placed just above the little yegg.

The Settlement, of course, was a better location for me than a hotel from every point of view. Quite apart from the curiosity that had brought me there, it offered great advantages. If in the weeks to come I got to be an object of interest to the police, and I might get that way quite innocently, the hotels would be combed, but the Settlement would never enter the official mind as the refuge of a crook. From the Hoboken terminal where they had been checked for the purpose I got my trunk and suitcase, and here I was, all set to see my search through to the end if I could discover a lead.

After one or two days of indecision I made up my mind that in order to be solid at the Settlement I'd have to become "engaged in art or professional work," as the desk-mistress had said. So during the day I was professionally engaged in the shoe business; that is, I was in a shop selling snappy brogues. My opportunities for investigation were only at night and on week-ends. I sometimes had to invent excuses to account for my customary absence, when some acquaintance I'd made suggested cards or a picture.

My fellow inmates would have been surprised if they had ever shadowed me. My inquiries took me north, south, east, and west, occasionally into the solemn spaces of the Public Library at Forty-second Street when I felt like digging for some trace of the names I wanted in directories and records, likely and unlikely. But generally my path lay among the squalid or garish precincts, in speak-easies and the lobbies of dollar hotels, in dance halls, around the docks and railroad yards, in joss houses and where the winter poor were found who slept on benches and on the grass in the sweltering nights of midsummer. I spent hours on street corners, and hung around the entrances of houses in the west Forties and east Nineties. The name Terry Fultz began to be known in a general way around Hell's Kitchen and Harlem.

6

Mr. Dockety's Departure

I WAS STAYING in one evening, for the look of the thing, talking to a young lawyer's clerk. We were in the so-called reception hall of the building, on the sixth floor. It was a long, low room, with broad alcoves, the whole place being given over in the evening to cards, petting, anagrams, radio and talk.

Then I had a glimpse, not more than that, of a tall, splendidly gowned woman, whose white face contrasted with the full black she wore. Her face—she was speaking to someone walking beside her—looked rather sad even while she talked and smiled. She passed our alcove and went out of the hall.

I looked at my companion. "She made an impression," I said.

"Why, don't you know who that is? That's Mrs. Gray Mason. She gave the money for this building. Rich, and how!"

"She must be."

"Terrible life, though, with that husband of hers, they say. She looks old."

"She's around fifty, isn't she?"

"Lord, no. Under forty."

At the same time that I kept my job at the shoe store and pursued my investigations at night here, there, and everywhere about Manhattan, I didn't forget my little protégé, the yegg.

He rejoiced in the name of Thomas Dockety and was supposed to be something in the varnish business. One day, overcome by violent curiosity—for I had again caught a glimpse of the yellow car on Fourteenth Street the night before—I called up the store and reported sick, and followed the yegg to business.

Sure enough, he went into a varnish factory on Twenty-fifth Street near the East River.

A few evenings I remained in my room after dinner. My door would be locked, my table drawn close under the lamp, and before me the photostated letters of Pat would be spread. I never tired of studying them in connection with Holborn's findings. When I considered the amount he had covered in the months between the time he took up the search and his death, I wondered if his thoroughness had left me any really promising ground to explore.

An agent he employed in England had attempted to trace Pat through the comic name, Philadelphia Boston. The Archery Company had been a sort of Cook's tours business, but the agent reported that the firm was dissolved. The books and records of the company were untraceable. As for identifying Dubrosky through some Russian city, where he had written his letter, the agent had declared the idea unthinkable.

I thought Holborn had done his cleverest work in connection with the reading Pat had done when her mother locked her in her room. In the one written report he had made to Aldrich, he said:

> From the way she squawked about the articles on patent medicine and fake cures in the magazines about that time, I figured that her folks must have made their pile in something like that. I'm going to check through the trade directories to see if the names of the poison manufacturers will be any help.

He had used Thomas's Register of American Manufacturers for the first year it was published, 1909, and he had listed all the firms he found there, not only those that had put out proprietary medicines, but the dealers in medical plasters and tablets and medicated lozenges and medicinal chemicals and extracts.

He then checked this list against the fakes hammered in the articles Pat had evidently read in *Collier's*. From her writing he didn't think that her people were concerned in the firms actually exposed in the articles, but he kept this open as a possibility. As to the remainder, some of them put out of business by Dr. Wiley under the Pure Food Act, Holborn conducted inquiries, painstaking and futile. He traveled hundreds of miles through the East and Middle West, and he wrote fake letters using names of people Pat had mentioned to see if this bait would bring up any fish.

In the end he had returned to New York City, convinced that there was only one thread left to try. He had made a memorandum of his intentions:

I'll have to get my hooks into one of the big shots. Sobey Wharton, Raffy the Guk, Boss Torrence—any might do. The best way is through the broads. I can make these babies work for me if I can get one framed on a statutory charge. I know a couple of frails who could turn the trick.

His conclusion was in line with my own early resolution to work through the underworld. I was going to enlist a big shot on my side too. My approach, however, would be friendly, not hostile. But that didn't mean less dangerous.

It must have been nearly one o'clock in the morning, and I was dressed for bed, lying on top of the spread, reading, when I heard a stir or commotion of some sort. I wrapped my old bathrobe about me and stepped into the hall, and then I knew that there were a lot of people on the landing of the floor below and a good deal of confused talking going on. They were mostly in dressing gowns and so forth, like me, but in the midst of the crowd I saw Miss Dilnay, the fussy little superintendent, fully dressed.

"Owtyougo, otttyougo, owtyougo!" she was saying, climbing nearer high C every time she repeated the phrase, and putting so much into the "out" that the rest was just a sneeze.

She was talking to a smooth little dark-haired girl, dressed in a man's overcoat and nothing else. She looked a little dazed and rather dogged, but I can't say that she was a bit ashamed.

"Yes, yes, *outyougo*," declared Miss Dilnay yet more emphatically. "You and Mr. Dockety too. *Out*-youbothgo, tonight. Outyougo, Miss Gabfuss, outyougo this very minute, if you please."

Then I caught sight of the little yegg in his suspenders as he raised his voice against the superintendent, slightly more ungrammatical than usual. "Rosey and me'll beat it, all right. Don't strain yerself. But you gotta give her a chance to get her shirt on, haven't ya?"

Miss Dilnay swelled to about twice her size after hearing this language.

The girl, who hadn't said anything, pushed her way through the crowd and down the stairs to the floor below. I thought that she gave a sort of flirt to the tail of the coat she wore in the direction of Miss Dilnay just as she commenced to go down the steps.

I whispered to someone to learn what it was all about, though a good deal was self-evident. What it amounted to was that the girl, whose room was on a different floor, was the sweetie of the little yegg, and that tonight, being quite lit, she had climbed up to his room, neglecting, however, to wear any clothing. By luck she reached his room unobserved, but then a quarrel had developed and she had wanted to go back without borrowing wraps. The yegg had tried to prevent her, and there had been voices raised just as Miss Dilnay passed the door. Her state of mind when she heard the mixed voices was bad enough, but it must have been indescribable when she boldly opened the door and saw what she saw.

She was master of the situation, however. In no time she had the girl encased in the yegg's overcoat and out into the hall where the crowd had gathered just before I came upon the scene.

I suddenly realized that this might be the very opportunity I was looking for. Only a couple of days before I had made inquiries at the license bureau about the number I had memorized from the plate of the big yellow car. And I knew, "varnish business" to the contrary, who the real boss of the little yegg really was.

I rushed back to my room and flung on my clothes. I had just put a soiled shirt in my laundry bag and I couldn't afford to take time getting studs and links into a fresh one. So I dressed without putting on a shirt, and turned up my overcoat collar to hide the neck of my pajamas.

Out on the pavement I looked anxiously for a taxi, which was an unlikely vehicle to be cruising in that part of Manhattan, especially at this hour. I didn't go far from the entrance of the Settlement for fear the yegg and his girl would walk out and disappear while I was absent. At length, just as they did emerge from the building, three cabs came along from the direction of Grand Street, all empty. A minute later I was once more following the little yegg through the streets.

It was only when the other taxi turned east on a street in the Fifties that I felt sure at last that the quarry was leading me somewhere, and for that contingency I had my plan prepared. I had recollected a story I had once read about a man who robbed a very exclusive club by appearing to the guests like a waiter and to the waiters like a guest. I saw how I could use the same dodge to get inside wherever the pair were going. If I failed, I could impersonate a drunk. Once inside—well, circumstances would tell. Aldrich paid me for taking chances.

By the time the taxi ahead had drawn in to the curb, I was out of mine, paying off the driver. By the time the couple had approached the street-level entrance of the gray stone house with black windows I was approaching the same entrance. When the door opened discreetly after someone had eyed us through a wicket, I stepped inside just as if I belonged with the little yegg.

The stupid, pugilistic-looking party who had admitted us into the dim hall said, "He was askin' for yuh today, Tom."

"Yeh," said Mr. Dockety. "We'll go up." He seemed a little nervous.

"O.K.," said the doorman.

The couple went up the narrow stairs, and I, who had stood at the elbow of the girl, followed close after.

My guides didn't pause at the first landing, but forged on up another flight. While climbing close behind them I heard voices through the big curtains that cut off the passageway from the rooms beyond. Once I thought I heard clicks that reminded me of a visit at Monte Carlo. Still ascending, I caught a glimpse through a space at the top of the curtains, of a room with a long table in it and a group of elegantly dressed people centering their attention on one end.

I recollected that the windows of this house were black.

We had reached the top landing and stood before the upper door, behind which were more voices, and much laughter. The couple stood there for a few seconds, the little yegg evidently in a funk. That obliged me to act. I reached between them and knocked.

The room we entered was lit from above by a bulb with a conical shade which cast most of the light down on the table beneath, filled with bottles and glasses. I had the impression of many faces, some vague outside the zone of light, some clouded in the haze of smoke that wafted toward the ceiling.

The yegg and the girl moved forward where the light fell upon them. I was still by the door, in obscurity.

I saw faces, many faces, but I had eyes for only one. Others I was aware of, one like a huge oyster with eyes and mouth, one mottled and scarred with disease, one broken-nosed, one a girl's face intensely pale and almost pinched, it was so bare of flesh, with narrow, intensely red lips and a subtle eye. That face grew clearer or dimmer as the smoke changed, but it was only one of those that formed a background for the laughing, youthful face in the center, the laughing face that had become so watchful, the young face with full blond hair combed back at top and sides, hair so luxuriant that the head was almost haloed in it.

He spoke in an even tone. "Whatya doin' here?"

The yegg and the girl whipped around then, and stared at me. I was still in the shadow, and they didn't recognize me.

"I dunno who he is," the little fellow gasped.

"I wasn't askin' *you,*" said the young man at the table. A little hubbub of talk arose, but he silenced it with a sharp gesture like a dagger thrust. He leaned across the table regarding me.

"Terry Fultz of Milwaukee. That's me," I answered, and out of my vest pocket I slipped a card I had had printed bearing that name, and flipped it onto the table before him. "I jus' found your front door open, Mr. Sabati, and I dropped in to have a little talk with you."

The lapels of my overcoat fell apart. He looked up from the card and saw my bare neck and the coat of my pajamas. Others saw the same thing, and the chatter broke out again. But I kept looking steadily at the young man. His eyes gleamed.

"Yeah? They must treatcha like hell in Milwaukee," he said.

7

Ratty the Guk

THE MOCKING, INSULTING GLEAM in his eyes—they were a vivid gray—died out. He jerked his head over his shoulder. "In there," he said.

I touched the knob of the door and it swung open. I couldn't see a thing beyond. A hand between my shoulder-blades compelled me to go on, even though a well might be ahead. I trod on what felt like a thick and expensive carpet and waited in the darkness.

A wall switch clicked and the room was illuminated with a pinkish glow. As I swung around I saw that it was a bedroom with luxurious curtains, an ivory toilet table, and a spacious half-canopied bed.

The young man with the bright gray eyes and the aureole of light hair was standing with his back to the door, watching me with a none-too-friendly expression. In his immaculate copper-colored suit with the small, fresh-looking rose in his buttonhole and the pale purple tie, he looked the picture of some matinee-idol or young theatrical producer. I answered his look with one just as steady.

He glanced at my card again. "Terry Fultz, yeah? What have I heard about you?" He snapped out his questions in slightly broken words I'm not trying to reproduce exactly here, this not being a thesis but a narrative.

"You might have heard I was in town, Mr. Sabati," I answered with thick politeness. "I was laying low awhile over in Jersey before I hit this burg."

"How do you know me?"

"I'd know you anywhere. Why, you're well known, Mr. Sabati. There's lots of people would know you anywhere." I nodded in the direction of his buttonhole with its strange adornment. "Your roses are famous."

"Yeah. Maybe that's right," he admitted, and an almost imperceptible expansion of his frame, quite unconscious, showed that he liked being well known. But he was keen and watchful. "You know me, but how do I know you? What the hell good is this?" He crushed the card between his fingers—sinewy, tapering fingers.

"You can look me up, check up on me, can't you?" I said peevishly. "You don't hafta believe me, do you?"

"You're from Milwaukee?" The question held a threat.

"Sure, around there," I answered, just managing to keep the sudden dryness in my throat from showing in my voice, as I forecast what was coming.

"You know Bull McCoy—Long Tom Gillinan?"

I had heard of these border rum-runners. "Sure—but not really know them. They worked a different racket."

"Yeah? What was your racket?"

"Jobs."

He looked me up and down. "Jobs? They're not so hot, boy. You get pinched for jobs sometimes, you know that?"

"Sure I do, I've done a stretch myself—in Madison."

"You come up here to talk, didn't you? Well, talk."

"I'm looking for a guy, and I need help."

"Yeah? So what?"

"I want your help, Mr. Sabati."

"You ain't gotcher nerve widya, sonny, no?" He made as if to spit disgustedly on the floor, but remembered the carpet.

"I know, but I got to find this bastard, and you could help me."

"Who?" The demand was sullen.

"Julian Sand, Clever Julian, they used to call him."

He was startled. For the first time he left his place at the door, moved into the center of the room. I stepped back as he came forward.

"Clever Julian!" he repeated. "What'de do, lay yer grandmother?"

"Oh, no, Mr. Sabati. He wasn't as old as that."

"But, Christ, why should I know him? He faded out before I ever—nobody ain't seen him round. Musta been bumped off long ago."

"He didn't croak," I declared with a toss of my head. "I want to keep a date with that old so-and-so."

"Well, I ain't stoppin' you. Why in hell pick on me?"

I admitted surprise. "Say, there's nothing you can't do with your line-up. It's better'n hiring the bulls to get your help, Mr. Sabati."

He rubbed his chin with the palm of his hand, vigorously; it seemed as if he had been struck by a deep thought. "You want me to locate Clever Julian for you? And you do jobs; that right?"

"Sure, that's right."

His eyes narrowed. "All right, Mr. Terry Fultz. I got something in your line. You do it for me, and I'll do my stuff for you. *Say!*" He took me by the shoulders, turned me part way so that my face was directly in the light. "You can put on the dog, too, can't you?"

"What—what do you mean?" I exclaimed in real surprise.

"You ever wore a dress suit?"

"Sure."

"Oh, boy!" He patted his chin with his fist several times, all thought. "Come in here tomorrow morning—no, make it Barker Street—down in the village. You know Barker Street?

It happened I did, from long ago.

"Twenty-one Barker Street, eleven thirty. Remember that number? Don't write it down."

"What am I, a freshman?" I said.

"Be there, and we'll talk." He jerked open the door into the room we had come from, and two beefy he-men fell away from the entrance. They must have had their ears glued to the cracks. "O.K., boys," he told them.

The crowd under the light and those outside its range were giving me a second once-over. A man off in one corner, tapping tunes with one finger on a baby grand, kept his face turned toward me. The girl with the white face and the thin red lips was smoking a cigarette in a jade holder. She didn't move her head, but her eyes turned toward mine. Later I found they were that most surprising and intriguing shade, cornflower blue. Her hair, black, shiny, was closely waved.

Mr. Dockety and Miss Gabfuss, otherwise Tom and Rosey, were sitting over by the wall. The young man turned his attention to them and asked with profane words what had brought them there. Tom explained how Rosey's visit had resulted. "But it was a terrible joint, Raffy," he pleaded. "I couldn't of stood it much more."

"It was a swell hole for anybody but a nitwit—and you get knicked out," retorted Raffy. "Tom, you dumb egg, if you queer any more of my plays, it'll be bad news."

"She got tight, didn't she? How could I help that?"

"Ah, you both make me sick," cried the young man. "Say, gang, you goin' to sleep here or something?"

There was a stirring and a scraping of chairs. Men and women rose and sifted. Then they stopped, everyone where he stood.

Somewhere outside near the head of the stairs, had sounded the clink of a bell, low but distinct, something like a cow-bell. Three strokes, then everything was still.

"Carson," declared Raffy with an oath. "That's Jack Carson again. What the hell does he think this is?"

"It's getting a habit with that flatfoot," said someone angrily. "Hell, three times this month—"

Feet were tramping up the stairs. The door to the landing, at which we all were looking, opened without a knock, and a man with a gnarled face and loose, dark clothing stepped in and closed it behind him, but the shadowy shapes of others had been visible while he entered.

"Evening," said the newcomer. "You need some ventilation here, Raffy."

"What's this about, Carson?" asked the young man sullenly.

"I'm just looking for Laxner," said the other softly. "Your friend Speed Laxner, the boy with the swivel hips." His rugged face, full of little knobs and valleys, had a hard, determined force in it. Yet his words were soft.

I had known who this gray-haired man was when his stooped, bunchy form appeared in the doorway. Jack Carson, Headquarters detective, assigned to most of the toughest jobs.

"Looking for Laxner!" exclaimed the young man in the brown suit, incredulously.

The detective nodded gloomily, as if in this world of woe this fact was the saddest thing of all. "Looking for Laxner, poor Speed Laxner," he repeated, and his eyes ran over the crowd. "Sorry to interrupt your party," he said.

"Just breaking up," said the young man.

"That's all right, then. I noticed that the game had closed downstairs."

"What game?"

"The game with the wheel and the little round ball. Didn't you know about that, Raffy? They play roulette on the floor below here sometimes."

"What's that got to do with me? I just rent this apartment."

"You're a cleverer man than your mother, Raffy," answered Jack Carson in the voice of a man of many sorrows.

"Lay off, Carson, lay off," cried Raffy the Guk with a dismissing wave of the hand. "You don't see Laxner here, do you? Well, beat it, then."

"I don't take orders from you, Raffy," returned Carson stolidly. "You may have the skipper of this precinct fixed, not me."

The detective gazed around the company once more. He muttered over some of their names, "Peru—Brophy—Phil—why Phil Hefner, is that you so modest over at the piano?"

The man sitting at the baby grand made some slight movement, probably of disgust at being recognized. Phil Hefner, the sensational song writer, almost rivaling Irving Berlin's success, with two shows on Broadway—picking out tunes with one finger!

"A bad place for young fellows like you," said Carson, drawing his mouth down at the corners. "Chaps like you and Wally Stemholzer there'll get in trouble if you play around with these boys and girls."

Stemholzer was evidently the lanky blond youth whose clothes rivaled Raffy's in elegance and who wore a disdainful look as a permanent fixture.

"Trouble, Stemholzer, trouble," repeated Jack Carson.

A couple of plainclothes men came through each of the other doors, having evidently made their way up by a rear staircase.

"He ain't here," said one of them.

Carson gave that tired, long-suffering nod. Already I was irritated by it; others who had endured it many times must have been infuriated. "Of course not, boys. They wouldn't keep a body here very long."

He turned on his heel and went out. The other detectives in the room and those on the landing tramped after him down the stairs.

There was a spell of silence as their steps died away. Then someone I had no handle to put to suddenly gasped: "My God, how did he know—how did he know Speed Laxner got blotted out?"

"Shut your trap!" hissed the young man in the brown suit, smashing his cupped hand across the speaker's mouth with a chaser of foul language.

The whole assembly seemed to take one long, deep breath, and just then the signal bell commenced again and gave seven slow, dull beats.

"That's the whole crowd of flatfeet," said someone.

Raffy fingered his chin, the thoughtful way. His voice was thick with hatred. "I'm gointa frame that dick some day, and when I do he'll stay framed!"

"Yeah," said the tall, slender, sneering youth I thought was Stemholzer, "and when he retires he'll write a book about it."

The interrupted break-up of the party proceeded. I got out of doors without saying anything to any of the others. Two or three cars parked up the block carried about half of them away. The big yellow bus I knew of was waiting when we reached the pavement, and the pale, dark-haired girl I had noticed—I believed I had heard her called Josephine—got in alone and the car purred away across town.

I felt satisfied with my night's progress. It had become obvious that I'd need help. The little yegg had taken me into the presence of a higher-up who could give me the very help I wanted.

Raffy the Guk!

Born Rafaello Sabati, and a few years back only a hanger-on on the fringes of his brother's vast network of organized gambling and specialized bootlegging, regarded as a lily and a weakling—now one of the most powerful racketeers in the East. The same night that saw his brother shot to death by a hop-head, saw the weakling seize his brother's place. It was a gruesome and decidedly bloody six hours between eleven and five, but at the end of it, there was Raffy firm on top!

I turned my coat collar up again as I entered the door of the settlement.

I did not go to bed immediately. Unlocking my trunk, I took out the photostated letters yet again and rapidly shuffled them over, selected one only and dropped the remainder back into the trunk. It was one of those belonging to the earlier group. One particular paragraph, bracketed by Holborn's pencil, was what I sought. I sat down on the bed and read it, perhaps for the hundredth time.

There's a Mr. Sand coming to dinner, and he's ever so clever. He's evidently a fad of father's, though mother says Heaven Forbid that such a man should break salt at our table. She said she would lock up the best silver if father persisted, but father laughed and said that the best isn't too good for Julian Sand. Mother boiled and declared that he mocked her. She is sure that Mr. Sand was a guest at the three house-partys that were robbed near us last spring. But Dubrosky—*she's afraid of more than the silver!* I'm sure she is, and I wonder what. One thing is certain. I will not be allowed to come to dinner tonight. So I shall come, of course, without being allowed. Father has yielded and will permit me to sit under the table with Terrence and share scraps with him. So I see at least the feet of clever Mr. Sand. . . .

There was no sequel to this episode in the letters. But pinned to the letter was a sheet half-filled with Holborn's blunt writing:

If this guest the old boy insisted on having for dinner wasn't Clever Julian, the smartest house thief of that time, I'm a sap. Maybe the old man knew his line before the police got wise, but cultivated him as a hobby. But Julian had a better line than robbery. He knew a lot of secrets that were expensive to keep. The police might be able to dig him up, or some big shot with a lot of finger men out working—unless he's buried too deep.

Buried too deep! That was what I was afraid of.

8

Room 328, Public Library

IT WAS a Sunday morning, so I didn't need to alibi myself at
the shoe store. I found Barker Street—it was really a cob-
bled alley hardly wide enough for a car to turn around—and
was outside the right number at five minutes to eleven. It
was a three-storied studio building.

Through a partly opened window that swung on a central
pin I caught a glimpse of a ground-floor bedroom with some
highly stabbing modernistic furniture, a bed on a dais with a
curious metallic-looking coverlet, and a toilet-table, all
angles, with a silver crucifix above it.

In the lobby only one of the bell-buttons could be pressed,
that belonging to the ground floor. The rest were empty
spaces. Later on I learned that Raffy paid the rent for all
three studios and kept the upper ones unfurnished. The
door-latch clicked, and I passed into the studio.

There seemed to be three main rooms on the ground floor.
The middle was the largest, and I was standing in it. It had
a blue plush carpet, one of the thickest I've ever stepped on,
and walls full of tapestries that even a tyro like me could tell
had cost big money. In the corner by the big window stood
an easel, palettes full of color lay carelessly beside it, and
the carpet was actually spotted and smeared with paints.
The picture on the easel was covered with a cloth, and a
good many canvases were standing with their faces against
the wall. Statuary, models of hands and heads and so forth,
and various jars and vases were standing wherever there
was room.

Opposite the door was a big divan, on which Raffy had
evidently been sitting with two girls I recognized from the
night before. One was the black-haired girl; the other was a
round-faced blonde, just a little passée and decidedly
listless. They faded toward the door of the room I had seen
from the outside.

While the door was closing behind them I saw more of
that pointed futuristic stuff inside, chairs that looked as

comfortable as spikes, a lamp consisting of three narrow black metal cylinders and a stiff black paper shade.

Raffy was still dressed like the boy idol of the screen or something, in a pearl-gray suit with a fresh pink rose in the lapel and he was smoking a long cigar in the manner of George Jessel.

"Good morning," I said.

He gave a queer look. "Yeah? I thought you'd show up."

"Show up? Why not?"

"They been trying to tell me you're a nose."

"Who has? Not your girl-friend."

"Hell, no! Some of the dumb heels I work with."

I folded my arms. "Well, why not?" I said calmly.

I meant him to be surprised. He didn't even remove his cigar. "Don't make me laugh. I judge men!"

"Yes? What makes you so sure about me?"

He waved the question away. "Take those pajamas, boy. No nose would have come in them—you didn't figure to do it yourself. Besides, no nose would have been dumb enough to crash my joint, anyhow, not without a stationful of cops. Carson brought six men, didn't he? And what the hell would you have been crashin' in for the night he come?" He laughed contemptuously. "You'd queered each other. And some of those bunnies want me to turn the heat on you!"

I was naturally interested in this. "I hope you fixed that all right, Mr. Sabati?"

"Sure I did. Don't you worry."

"Because I'd be sorry if anything happened to them, Raffy," I said softly. "You might be sorry to miss one or two of 'em if they was good men."

He looked at me intently, puffing a time or two.

Then, "Lay off the rough stuff," he grunted, dropped his cigar into the nearest vase, and moved nearer.

He outlined his scheme in a few rapid sentences. I wish I could equal his conciseness.

There was a man named Gray Mason he wanted watched. (A rumble of memory came to me on hearing that name.)

I was to meet him, gain his confidence, get invited to his house, learn as much as I could about him. Then—here Raffy hesitated before making up his mind to tell me what next. I suspected that the confidence game would be tried. But it was otherwise. Raffy gazed at me keenly and said that there might be a robbery at Gray Mason's house if I made good. There were papers Raffy wanted.

"If we have to bend 'em, you'll go along, see? But maybe we can get 'em without a regular job." It was no good attempting the robbery before I learned the geography of the house.

What can a man do? I was thinking while all this was coming up. I knew I'd come to the wrong place if I wanted to stay technically straight. I couldn't run with both hare and hounds. I was in a web. What can a man do? Retire gracefully, I suppose. But that was morally impossible at this late date.

"Follow him up, get the idea?" Raffy was saying. "Get a line on him, see? He'll surprise you, brother."

"What kind of a guy is he?"

"Society—top step," declared Raffy. "So you gotta be careful, see? Work up to him, get me?"

"But how the hell can I make a guy like that?" I burst out, thinking it well to show a certain amount of reluctance to attempt what I felt would not actually be very hard. "What *is* this bird? What's he do?"

"Those bozos don't do nothin'," he assured me with a wave of the hand.

"Then how the—"

"Wait a minute, wait a minute. Get this. He don't do nothin', but he has a hobby. See?"

"Go on."

"Well, you'll make him through this hobby. That's easiest."

"A hell of a help that is!" I said bitterly. "How am I going to work if I don't know what this hobby is, or where—?"

"I'll give you all that," he promised. "You'll get a load o' the dope, all right."

He shouted, and a moment later the two girls entered from the bedroom. Raffy indicated the blonde one, rather with a nudge of his shoulder than with the words he used. She had come back from the bedroom all bright and cheery, a different woman.

"Linna Cabwen's going to work with you," said Raffy carelessly. "That's if you need her." He spoke to her. "You better be 'round tonight, kid."

"Sure," said Linna. She shot a quick look at me, and I caught a glimpse of a smile in her eyes, something mocking, contemptuous, yet light.

"Now get this," said Raffy, pulling out his watch, worth about a thousand. "I ain't got but two-three minutes. So get me, and don't make me talk twice. Fultz, you begin tonight on Mason. You know the Public Lib'ry—I mean at Forty-second Street?"

"Sure, I went in there once," I said.

"You can pick him up there tonight. Room 328. He goes there Sundays regular."

I had been in that very room too, plenty of times, but I didn't let him see it.

"What's he like?"

"You get there early and look at the register. It's up to you. Chase him home."

"My God, don't you even know where he lives?" I exclaimed. I didn't need to manufacture that surprise.

"Sure, I think I do. He's been tailed before. But how do I know the bums that worked on him weren't cock-eyed?"

"He's not in the phone book?" I asked incredulously.

"Hell, no, private number. You'll have to work on this bird."

"O.K.," I assured him crisply.

Raffy nudged toward the light-haired girl again. "Linna better be waiting for you outside the lib'ry. If he goes somewheres you may want a dame with you." He said to the girl, "Spoke'll drive you in the Buick, baby."

"What time?" she asked.

"Six." Raffy was in front of a mirror, turning down the brim of his snappy velour. "Spoke'll park in Fifth Avenue right up front. He'll be there till you come out, Fultz. Can't miss him, boy. The street's empty around that time. O.K., baby?"

"Sure," Linna agreed.

Raffy and I walked out together. The dark girl had kept herself in the background. I hadn't heard her voice or learned her name, but once or twice I had caught the intense gaze of her oddly tinted eyes.

The big yellow car came up and took Raffy away.

I was well heeled and had on my best outfit when I stepped into Room 328 that night. The Genealogy Room is at the north end of the third floor, and you pass through the big central Reading Room to get to it. I took a book from one of the few open shelves, sat down at one end of the room, and covertly examined the people there.

I went to the desk to sign up, taking a long time to do it with a bad pen, and noting every name on the evening register. There was no Gray Mason there, but that proved nothing.

Two or three more came in while I circled around the tables, and just as I reached the register again, a small clawy hand was writing "Gray Mason, 1 E. 68."

He was a slight chap, middle-aged or more, sharp as a hatchet, with the skin stretched tight across the mouth and chin but wrinkling toward his eyes and ears. He wore striped trousers and a short black coat. I wouldn't have looked at him twice if it hadn't been for those eyes. They were small and glittered, some dark shade.

I chose a seat just across from him and tried to seem immersed in my book. He worked very fast and intently with one of those yellow pads of scratch-paper in front of him, and his pencil constantly at his bloodless lips, which soon became discolored. He had only two books before him, and he constantly compared some page in one with a page in the other.

His eyes occasionally lifted; he was watching the clock. At length he glanced at his watch, closed the books, put his pad in a brief-case, picked up his hat and slipped out.

I stayed only long enough to glance at the names of the two volumes he had been comparing. I got the first of several quick surprises that evening. One was "The History of Lincoln County, Massachusetts," harmless enough. The other was "The Brovard Family."

My head was spinning while I followed him through the huge reading room and down the marble hallways. "The Brovard Family!"

9

The Hobby of Gray Mason

OF COURSE IT MIGHT BE only a coincidence that the Brovard case was on then. It didn't get quite as much tabloid publicity as the Hall-Mills and Gray-Snyder affairs that had preceded it and whose place it had taken in the newspapers, but I always thought that was because the Brovard woman had chosen to abolish her man during the day instead of at night, like Mrs. Snyder and Judd Gray and the unknown killers near the pig woman's farm.

And here was the mysterious Gray Mason studying the family tree of Madeleine Brovard's husband. What did that mean?

He went out onto the broad plaza that fronts Fifth Avenue. I followed, looking up and down the block for the Buick containing the blonde. Mason stood on the curb, looking up the dark avenue, evidently intending to snag a taxi.

I headed for the only Buick in sight. The man at the wheel was a stranger to me, but that didn't hinder me from approaching and looking in. I recoiled then, for though there was a girl, she wasn't the blonde.

But the door was opened from inside. "Come on in," said a voice I didn't recognize, from the dark interior. The driver seemed to expect me to do the same. Then the girl's face appeared at the window, and I knew her for the pale-cheeked, thin-lipped brunette.

"What's the matter?" she asked. "Aren't you coming?"

I got in at once, saying, "What's the idea? I thought—"

"Linna don't feel so well," said the girl. "She's trying to beat the dope, you know, so I came instead."

I wasn't surprised, after a moment. The faded blonde had at first looked like an addict, and she had later come out of the bed-room like a dope who had just had a snifter.

The girl asked, "What do we do? Did you spot him?"

I leaned forward. "I'll say I did. Look there." I pointed at the slight, dapper figure then about to enter a taxi.

"Trail the cab, Spoke," called the girl, and the Buick started with a jerk that threw me partly across the body of my companion. I straightened myself up with an apology as she laughed.

It wasn't a long trail. Gray Mason paid off the taxi-driver at the McAlpin, and went inside. Before we could get in to the curb, I leaped out and dashed into the lobby. Gray Mason wasn't there. I looked into the passage where the elevators were: not there either.

The girl had joined me by now. "He must have gone downstairs," I said. "There's a grill room down below. We'll try that."

At the entrance to the grill we waited on a sofa by the wall of the ante-room. Sure enough, in a couple of minutes the man came briskly toward the entrance. I turned toward the girl to prevent him getting a look at me. That act enabled me to see that he paused at the threshold of the grill and looked the diners over very carefully before choosing a table. He was still carrying his briefcase.

We got up and went inside and I managed to get the table I wanted after almost coming to blows with the headwaiter. Gray Mason was in a somewhat secluded position beside one of the big stone pillars that made the place resemble a crypt. The pillar stood between him and the dance floor. We sat beside the next pillar, behind him and further from the floor.

Until the girl removed her wrap I hadn't had a chance to see how elegantly she was dressed, without any vulgar display. She wore a black scoured silk with a scarlet rosette at the shoulder and a thin line of scarlet ran down across her breast. Her eardrops were red stones that held living sparks. Her face was pale and cold. Her black hair shone like marble. In my ordinary dark suit, alongside her I must have looked like something left over from the day before.

We ordered and ate. "By the way," I said. "It might help if I was to know your name."

"Josephine. That's my name." Yes, I remembered now, Raffy had called her Josie the night before.

"And that's all?"

Her other name was Cecchi. She explained at some length (to one ignorant of Italian) how it was spelled and why. "But you're not going to call me Miss Cecchi, are you? Don't kid me."

"How long have you known Raffy?"

"Oh, a couple of months. Why?"

"Because—I don't see what the hell business he has staying away if he's only known you a couple of months."

My speech, for better or worse, was too direct and sincere for her to laugh off. She looked aside; one corner of her mouth turned up in a way that might have meant anything. Her profile was clearcut, straight nose, faultless forehead.

As we were finishing dinner, I wondered how we could prolong our stay in case Mason stayed. There was dancing, of course, but I wanted to sit where I was. I was a rotten dancer—and suppose Mason walked out while we were on the floor?

But mostly I was curious about Mason's behavior. He had taken newspapers out of his brief-case, and they littered his table. He had some folded and leaning against the pillar beside him, others propped against his water-jug and bowl of flowers. He appeared to any unsuspicious observer to be examining these papers. What he was really doing was watching the diners at the table to the right of his.

Two old sports and two girls occupied that table, and they were having a royal party. I never saw a board loaded with so many kinds of expensive food. One man was getting on in years and apparently wore a white wig. He supplied most of the conversation and seemed to be a humorist. The other was a youngish chap much heavier, who smoked cigarettes and smiled through the whole meal. Both had very red faces.

The girls—well, Josephine and I had mentioned them earlier in the evening. We had agreed on one thing. As Josephine put it, "There can't be any question about them being respectable!"

The dancing went on under colored tints reflected from a glass globe above the dancing floor. Sometimes the colors were switched off, and there was a blaze of intense white light.

During one of these flashes at the end of a dance, I was sure I heard a faint metallic scraping from the table ahead of ours. For the remainder of our stay I kept my eyes constantly on the movements of Gray Mason. I became absolutely certain that he was taking a series of photographs of the men and the girls. A small camera was concealed in his left sleeve, and he utilized the occasional intervals of bright light.

A few minutes later Mason decided to go. His waiter gave him his check, and later his change, and he went out. I hadn't been able to flag the man who served us, but I signaled Josephine it was time to step. I threw down a yellow greenback to cover the charges and had to return from the door of the grill to recover it, as I had left a hundred-dollar bill by mistake.

The girl had hurried on up to the lobby, to keep an eye on Mason if possible. I saw her at the top of the stairs. "He's leaving."

We almost lost the taxi that contained Mason. It was easy to follow, however. At one stop, just before entering Central Park, Spoke leaned back and talked through the window. "I can take you ahead of him."

"What do you mean, ahead of him?" I asked.

"I trailed this bird before. He lives over on the Avenue."

So it proved. Gray Mason probably roamed no more that night. On Fifth Avenue, at Sixty-eighth Street he dismissed his cab, and went inside the heavily grilled entrance of a house with a marble front.

Somehow, though it was only a fool notion, I had a vision of him hastening into some part of the house where there was a dark room, and I saw him working in the dim red light on the tiny roll of film. What was he after? Was it possible that this man could extort money from the men? I couldn't see it, somehow. Was he framing the girls? That seemed even less likely—no point to it. For there was no doubt what they were. For the time the real secret of Gray Mason was beyond my grasp.

"Youse don't want me no more?" asked Spoke.

"What's the big idea?" I said.

"I got a date."

"Sure, bounce away," said Josephine; I thought she was snatching at the opportunity. "We'll taxi to the Village."

So that left us standing under an arc light. "Now where do we go?" she said.

I wouldn't have minded if she'd wanted to be taken home and let it go at that. But so far, of course, it had been practically no evening at all for her. And the late pictures hadn't even started.

"We'll go to the Roxy and then some place we can dance," she said, when I asked her to suggest something.

"I'm a rotten dancer," I told her.

Her fingers reached out narrow and white across the side of her wrap. "What are you trying to do, ditch me?" I met her eyes.

"Do I look like a sap?" I asked. "It's not what I want—"

"Getting chicken on account of Raffy?" she mocked. "Well, we can go some place where they don't know us, can't we?"

I couldn't let her think that my whole objection was on account of losing my sleep. We saw the show at the Roxy and danced until three a.m.

While the hours passed in that rather quiet Harlem night club, and the music did everything it could to make me happy because I was there and had this girl with me, and while I began to get less clumsy as Josephine went for miles around the polished floor in my arms, a faint tinge of color appeared in her white cheeks, the first I had seen. It was not always, but only in the midst of some particularly languorous music that this flush appeared. It showed through the delicate texture of her skin, never actually coming to the surface but hovering beneath. Then she smiled, and her eyes, generally closed, opened, and her look met mine. With her no one could help dancing well.

We talked. I asked her where she had met Raffy. "At Loft's," she said. "I was working there."

I hardly know now which I had more right to be surprised at, her simple admission of working behind a candy counter, or Raffy visiting Loft's.

Riding home with her, I said, "Where is he tonight?"

She shrugged her shoulders. "Out on the road, he told me. Somebody's paying off. Take it or leave it."

"I don't want to be fresh, understand," I said. "But what do you do in this studio of yours? Paint?"

"I don't paint. Wally comes and does sometimes when Raffy's not crabby. I throw parties there sometimes."

I meant to ask her more about this Wally, but we were there by that time. I left her on the doorstep.

An Eighth Street crosstown car dragged almost to the door of the settlement. I had many things to think of and keep we awake on the trip, memories of Josephine floating in my arms, a stubborn sense of mystery in Gray Mason's photography—but greatest of all, somehow, was the Brovard Family History.

Though I went places and did things with Linna Cabwen too, that was not the last time that Josephine and I went out together. If the other girl was dopey, and Raffy wasn't on tap, Josephine would join me for an evening of quiet pastime. Twice again we trailed Mason, without results. When I was at Raffy's with the crowd, I would sometimes see the cornflower-blue eyes studying me, puzzled, their own shade a puzzle enough to drive a man wild if he didn't have his feet firmly on the ground.

Once, I remember, as we came home silently in a cab, she suddenly said, "He don't own me, you know."

"What do you mean?" I said.

"Oh—nothing." It was as if she was grinding her teeth.

10

Meeting the Murderess

MEANWHILE I MADE Gray Mason. It took weeks, in the course of which I gave up working at the store, since I needed to watch the residence, follow the man when he came out, find his interests and connections. He spent his days and some evenings largely in the Library, going out to dine at seven-thirty or so, carrying his briefcase, watching people.

Then one evening I found the cheese for my mousetrap. I had trailed him a couple of times to the Central Athletic Club before I found out what his interest there was. Prowling past the windows, I caught sight of him. With a green shade over his eyes, and a mammoth of a man for opponent, he was playing checkers.

Now I had once been something of a checker-player myself, highschool champion, in fact, and I had continued to study the game. So one evening in the Library I took out my small pocket board and laid out an interesting position, and became terribly engrossed in it. He came in presently, and I knew he was watching me. But it wasn't until the next time that I caught a glimpse of his striped trouser-leg beside me, and heard him say, in a soft and reedy voice, "Beg pardon, but you seem to be interested in draughts."

I evinced no surprise, but inside I was chortling and chuckling. For I knew I had him then.

A beautiful friendship began between us, and it wasn't long before I "discovered" that he was interested in the Brovard family. I let it be seen that I was working on Rhode Island local history, and that a mystery was connected with my investigation.

He asked me if I'd care for a bout of "draughts," as he persisted in calling the game. "You can tell me more about your Rhode Island problem."

I told him my game was rusty, very rusty, but I didn't lose the opportunity to accept. He was as curious as a squirrel about my work, and I sensed that dirt would make him happy.

During the month I had bought myself some new clothes to match his rich ones, and I was groomed to go anywhere with him without exciting comment.

The Brovard trial, in the meanwhile, dragged on, but on the evening I dined with Mason at the Central Athletic Club it looked as if the prosecution couldn't drag it out much farther. Already half a dozen lovers had been linked with Madeleine Brovard.

Over the meal I unbosomed myself completely about the "work" I was doing in the Library. I gave him a long, involved story about Rhode Island families named Deeds and Tallentyre and the Civil War—put on an act of referring to a memorandum book—brought out a "secret" of a suppressed will. I had him fascinated, all right.

Then we played, and I, with some trepidation, moved the first piece. But the game went along lines I was familiar with, and I forced him continually. He was lucky to draw. And while we were playing, I had another brilliant idea. The Draughts and Counters Club!

When I mentioned it, he pricked up his ears, and his eyes gleamed. He *had* heard of it, was bursting to visit it.

I said, "But after all, what is it, Mr. Mason? Only a group of men playing checkers in a basement room."

"Yes," he breathed. "But *such* men!"

I believe it was the Draughts and Counters Club that swung the balance.

And three days after I promised to take Matson there, Madeleine Brovard was acquitted. The tabloid public's judgment was vindicated.

She had, of course, gone to Abe Johnson's office and waited for him and shot him three times with great deliberation and careful aim as he entered and before he said a word. But the defense showed that Johnson wasn't much of a hero, and Madeleine declared she had been quite fussed before and after the shooting. You can't deny the force of facts like these in an American court of law.

She and her husband, with whom she had apparently been reconciled, disappeared toward the end of that week.

The evening came when Mason and I were to have dinner together and go to the Draughts and Counters at nine. Tonight, as I told him, a blindfold exhibition would be in the program.

There were about twenty men in that smoke-filled basement room. The blindfold player announced his moves from beneath a sack-like mask which had a black tape wound around the eyes. He spoke in a coarse voice, and occasionally coughed thickly.

In the room was a collection of desperadoes and dope-fiends with but a single bond: their love of the game of checkers. Some had learned the game under railroad trestles or in prison camps, or perhaps in parlor houses. One, I knew, had studied combinations while under sentence of death, before his reprieve and pardon.

We had hardly been seated among the spectators on one of the semi-circle of benches and got used to the haze of cigar-smoke when there was an interruption—a permanent interruption.

A shot rang out and the turbid atmosphere was lit by a brief burst of fire. I had seen the hand with the gun in it, and Mason and I had crashed to the floor together. As I struggled to an upright posture, I saw two or three men hanging onto the blindfold expert's arm.

We were nearest the door; in no time I had urged Mason through it and up the stairs to the street. We walked rapidly toward the nearest corner, leaving the sounds of struggle behind.

"My dear fellow, how extraordinary!" he said. "What possible motive could he have had for shooting at you?"

"I can't imagine."

I couldn't imagine because there wasn't any. For when I had fallen against Mason, I had knocked him out of the path of the bullet. Blink Handy, with whom I had played many a time at Franklin and to whom I owed our admission, had tried to kill Gray Mason. The blindfold expert was my old opponent the trusty.

Mason said, "Shall we inform the police of this?"

"Only if you want to get put on the spot."

Presently Mason offered another observation. "But then he wasn't blindfolded at all."

I said, "Not likely."

And five days later I had use for my newly-fashioned dress suit. I had succeeded beyond my hopes, and was crashing right into the Mason mansion itself!

It took as much courage for me to climb the stairs of Mason's Fifth Avenue residence as it had to crowd my way to the top floor of Raffy's gambling place. The bit of pasteboard in my pocket, talisman that had admitted me through the double-grilled gates at the entrance at 68th Street had a certain ominous-ness in its message, which I knew by heart:

"Gray Mason requests the honor of (here my name was inserted in the man's handwriting) attendance on the evening of April 15 to meet Madeleine Brovard and her husband. Only the right people will be present."

Real marble stairs. "Only the right people will be present." Well, I'd see what that meant.

It was a gaudy crowd. The outside tints had been laid on pretty thick; a wronger-looking set could hardly have been collected. The young-old, the old-young, the gay-sad, and the sad-gad—all were there, and not one seemed genuinely at ease, nor did any of them seem to think it strange for Mason to give a party for the murderess.

Madeleine Brovard was, I think, one of the most ordinary and innocuous women, to look at, that I had ever met. The baby-faced little gun-woman had baby-blue eyes and enamel-pink cheeks. Her husband was not a pleasant specimen, being tall and ungainly with unkempt red-brown hair; his cranium was square and inhuman. He had a greasy face and a thick but untrained bristle on his upper lip.

I hadn't much more than a word with Mason, but he seized the chance to ask me about the Deeds-Tallentyre tangle, on which I had to report progress. I was slightly worried about this, for I might have to produce some documentary proof one of these days to keep him credulous, and I resolved to have the goods ready, with a good strong story. But, as it proved, the imaginary Deeds and their hated Tallentyres were never to be trotted out again.

I knew one thing, anyhow, after that brief interview. My invitation to this shady affair had the main purpose of nursing me along. I could see that the instant he thought of the Deeds and Tallentyres his imagination was alive.

One gambit I thought I'd try, when I had a chance to say a word to the Brovard wench as she returned from a brief excursion. Could I bring the light of feeling into those baby-blue eyes? I took her aside, whispered, "I think you're in danger."

"Danger? What do you mean? Me?" It was an absolutely stereotyped reaction: incredulity, verging on derision.

"I do. Don't tell anyone, *anyone,* understand?"

She laughed, rather weakly, tried to break away. I went on with the farce. "Can't you think of anyone here who'd want to harm you? Aren't any of these people your friends?"

" I never saw a one of them before, only the Masons and that Countess woman."

"And how did Mason get you here?"

"What d'you mean, Mister? Say, who you think—oh, well he said we could escape from publicity this way."

"Yeah?" I thought this style went better with her. "You're a sap. Can't you think of any way, any special way, anyone might harm you? Something to do with your family, per-haps?"

It was a telling shot. "No, no!" she exclaimed again, and I knew she meant Yes. Then I let her go, having brought at least a trace of emotion to that mechanical toy.

Alone for a moment, I admired the opulence and splendor of Mason's home. The decorations showed the thoughtful choice of someone, Mrs. Mason, I supposed. "All thrown away on a set of bounders and bitches," I said to myself. But what was their common denominator? Why in par-ticular were they Gray Mason's guests?

The women matched the men, but one, whose name had come to me clearly and who had made a somewhat other impression was the Countess de Sieffert, a small but very active woman. Of uncertain age like the rest, her face was a coat of many colors, with lips splashed an inch red, above which flamed a great globe of snaky hair, all orange-yellow. She wore jewelled eardrops as large as half-dollars. She spoke rapidly with little gestures and a trace of accent, in-definite as to nationality. I thought her eyes, dark grey, had a hardness that didn't quite belong to her for all her pea-cock makeup. She was apparently Mrs. Mason's only friend in the crowd.

I now saw Mrs. Mason for the second time, the first having been the night she was pointed out to me at the Settlement her money had endowed. Tall and slender, she would have been impressive anywhere, and she loathed this company. Her face gave off no light, any more than the pearls she wore. I got the notion that Mason had planned the party without consulting her.

There was to be a picture shown in the projection room further upstairs at half an hour before midnight. From some of the remarks I overheard, the guests were expecting pornography (*"She* won't be there," said one hussy with a contemptuous flirt toward Mrs. Mason), but it was not to be. Instead Mason had dug up a melodrama from the semaphore era of movie acting, "Passion's Golden Dye," concerning a brother and sister who plotted against a distant relative for his money. Just as I slipped out and down through the emptied rooms, the precious pair were plotting to pose as husband and wife, to lure the victim into the girl's clutches and bleed him.

The servants and all were resting or feasting, the gods be thanked! I trotted downstairs to the small cloakroom to the right of the entrance where the men had left their gear. The sole window was narrow, but it would admit me or a larger person. A metal shutter was outside.

I had four things to do. I had to oil both window and screen. I had to tamper with both the catch and burglar alarm, if any. I found the alarm, and standing on the footman's chair I cut the wire where it made a turn under a tack-head, which concealed the cut. With a small folding screwdriver and a couple of dummy screw-heads I made the safety-catch useless. With a tiny can of oil I made the sash work silently. Opening the window, I oiled the sides of the shutter. Then I got out of there damned quick, relieved.

One more chore, Gray Mason's room. I had noted which corridor he had appeared from in the midst of the party, and I soon found which suite was his.

I slipped in quickly, stood inside, my back to the door. My fingers sought the switch; there was a flood of light. I reconnoitered. The room had a thick green carpet, tacked down along all the baseboards. There was a flowered paper on the wall. The place contained the kind of furniture I had expected, expensive but not showy chairs, bed, and dresser. No bookcases. On a broad table beside the window was a hooded typewriter with various kinds of paper jutting out from a small cabinet to the right.

Three rooms opened from the bedroom, a closet, a bath and a dark room. Superficially none promised what I wanted.

Ten minutes' rapid prying and poking revealed nothing. Then I stood on the radiator above which hung one of those paintings which is mostly frame, and pulled the picture away from the wall. There was a door there, perhaps twenty inches square. I had found what I wanted.

Now the odd thing happened. As I made my way upward to the projection room on the fourth floor I heard the whistled catch of a tune from the room at the head of the third flight. It was a bit from Gilbert and Sullivan's "Ruddigore." A little recklessly I went over and put my eye to the keyhole, and saw the Countess de Sieffert, in her costume half feathers and every shade of the rainbow, bending over a bed on which lay the contents of somebody's valise.

She wasn't hurried at all, and hearing her do that tune so gaily took ten years from her age for me.

Then the house seemed to quiver, or my knees suddenly became universal joints, and out of control.

There was an agonizing scream from upstairs. A moment later I was conscious that the Countess was standing beside me on the landing. But my greater consciousness was of the flood of feet pouring down the stairs, the furious flood, the voice that rose above it all in terror: "He made me! He made me!"—a woman's voice bubbling, choking, fighting to be a voice, and coming out in a fine-drawn wail. "He made me swallow it."

The flood burst into a nearby room, and those who were carrying her laid Madeleine Brovard down on the bed.

I jammed my way inside, saw the girl writhing there; someone, perhaps with medical knowledge, bawled for milk, for eggs, for mustard and water. Then suddenly the body ceased its throes, the whistle in the windpipe died down. One last bubble of foam appeared on the lips, and broke. The murderess was dead.

The nightmare went on. What I remember best was the look of Jack Carson's boot-toes sinking into the carpet downstairs where most of us were huddled.

Someone told what had happened in the projection room, and we all acquiesced, even I, who had not been there. It was agreed:

That at a certain point in the showing of "Passion's Golden Dye" there had been a muttered dispute in a certain part of the audience. That no one had paid heed to the interruptions, thinking that an extra drink or two accounted for them. That there were sounds of a struggle. That the struggle had been followed by a shriek, and after the lights went on, by another, from the lips of Madeleine Brovard, who vas then twisting in agony on the floor. That she had pointed, or tried to point, at her husband. That she had been carried down the stairs into her room and placed on the bed where she died. That while being carried downstairs she had uttered the words I had heard. That Teddy Brovard had been searched, and a small bottle, recently emptied, found in his pocket. That the bottle gave off a strong disagreeable odor.

I can remember, though, a moment's look that passed between Mrs. Mason and her husband. Such blazing, raging eyes I never hope to see again. Their hatred was loathing. Under that withering glare, he remained unwithered. In his eyes the glitter seemed to grow.

11

The Housebreakers

THE THREE OF us sat in Raffy's place on Fifty-seventh Street without any light except the shaded wall-lamp.

"Never mind what it's a picture of," snarled Raffy. "It's a picture, see? If you find it you'll know it, see?"

"I get you," I answered. "You're in it."

He didn't look so handsome with his face pulled all over to one side. "Maybe I am, maybe not. But you'll know it when you see it, get me? And boy, oh boy, you bring it here right away."

I said, "If you're so damned anxious to have it that you're afraid I'll be bumped off with it on me, why don't you go after it yourself?"

His jaw stuck out, and he spoke almost without moving it, emphasizing with little jerks of his left hand. "I took plenty risks, Terry. I took plenty risks. Now you want me to find Clever Julian for you, eh? But you do this for me first, eh?"

"Sure," I drawled. "I'll get it for you, Raffy. I'll have it here before the peep of dawn. Keep the wool on."

Raffy turned to the man sitting at his left, who in the dimness looked the color of an old leather binding. "Peru, he'll bring it, get me?"

"Yeh," said Peru, who had few words.

So although I was the leader of the expedition, Peru was going to supervise me. After all, I was Terry Fultz, newcomer. Was Raffy suspicious?

"What's he got to do with it?" I demanded. "You heard me say—"

"Shut up, you!" Evidently Raffy's nerves were frayed. The picture business must mean a lot to him, a tremendous lot. Then he said suddenly, "Remember, you Terry. *Don't croak Mason!* Peru, get that!"

"No danger," I said: "No hot seat for me."

"You do anything else," said Raffy. "Cripple him if you got to, but, boy, oh boy, if you croak him, you won't have to wait for the hot seat. I'll fix you!"

Two o'clock had just struck as we set out from Raffy's.

The home of Gray Mason, with its two stories of granite laid in big oblong blocks, with two stories of brick above, stood on the south corner and had its entrance on Sixty-eighth Street. On the north corner a vast unfinished apartment house had a much larger frontage extending halfway down the block. The lower floor of this new building was barricaded, but sheds and roofed passages made it easy to find cover there. Half the street was filled with crated bathroom fixtures, bags of cement, piles of sand, loose planking.

Traffic was passing in Fifth Avenue, but by transferring a couple of red lanterns from the crated goods and cement bags to boxes which we placed in the middle of the entrance to the street we made certain that no car would turn into Sixty-eighth Street from that direction. I selected a short, strong plank from those that were loose.

Gray Mason's house was separated from the sidewalk by an unusually deep well that extended moat-like around three sides of the structure. We placed one end of the plank on the sill of the window I had prepared, and the other end on the railing above the moat. No one passing on the Avenue could see anything amiss, as the entrance-way, glassed in opaquely, was between us and the thoroughfare and made a good screen.

We were much more direct and quick than I have been in description. We crossed the street with the plank, set it up, climbed over the sill, pried open the steel shutter and the sash inside, climbed in, and pulled the plank inside after us, all in about two minutes. We closed the shutter, but not the window. Soon, disguised with loose cloth masks, we were on our way through the larger spaces of the house.

It was an easy place to get about in, even without an occasional use of Peru's torch. The plan of the rooms was simple, and every foot was carpeted, so our rubber soles were hardly necessary. Yet it was with a hurried heart that I guided my companion down the corridor to Gray Mason's room, and I realized that there was an idiotic prayer on my lips when we reached the door. The prayer was that the door shouldn't be locked.

My hand found the knob, which turned silently, and the door opened at the least push. I had been holding my breath, and I almost let out a huge explosive sigh of relief.

Inside the room, it looked as if the bed was empty. Peru gave one quick flash to make sure. The covers had not even been turned down.

"What did I tell you?" I whispered in Peru's ear. "The report was right. He's away tonight. Say, the shades are even drawn. He won't be back."

"Show us the safe," he growled in a whisper of his own.

In the corner at the side where I had found the safe was a standing lamp. I lit it. A corner screen concealed a telephone. Next to the screen the radiator squatted, and the safe was just above.

Peru and I stood on the radiator and got the picture down, and then he examined the little door which had lain behind.

"Chubb lock," he said with a suppressed oath.

"Got to force it?"

"Yea. Next room?"

"Nobody in it before."

"O.K." He drew from an inner pocket a steel bar with one end tapering and a rubber cap at the other, also a short, heavy hammer. Inserting the sharp end in the crevice of the door, above the lock, he hammered with soundless strokes.

I left him, and began to search among the papers on the typewriting table. There was an enormous supply of unused typewriting paper, also a good deal of carbon paper, but not a trace of anything typed. The safe seemed to be the only hope.

Peru beckoned. He had made use of another jimmy, and the two levers had almost conquered the door. Of several methods, including the cutting away of the lock, he had chosen that least likely to result in an alarm.

With one concerted wrench we tore the door open, and the noise was not as great as I had feared. A little green safe, one of the kind with rounded corners, squatted in the cavity.

We pulled it out—it was not fixed in place, but rather heavy—and lowered it carefully to the floor. It had both a lock and a combination. Peru twirled the knob a couple of times. He snorted, and I think he suppressed a contemptuous laugh.

While he worked happily and confidently on the combination—even I heard the tumblers clink—I was struck by a subtler problem than the one he pursued.

What was the meaning of a difficult lock on a door protecting a safe it was child's play to open?

I was still in need of an answer when Peru, satisfied, took out a small bunch of skeleton keys, and inserting one, unlocked the safe with the first twist. The door swung open.

Photographs—the inside was crammed with photographs. They came tumbling out on the carpet, and piles remained, photos by the score, all three by five, fastened in neat packets. Peru pulled out the last of them. The back of the cavity appeared; it had contained nothing but photographs. No documents.

The picture we wanted: Raffy had said, "You'll know it when you see it." Peru's hands and mine went to work.

In a minute our glances met, in three minutes I heard Peru's heavy breathing, in ten he was cursing none too softly under his breath in a steady stream of foulness. We both leaned back on our haunches, backs weary from strain, and looked at each other again. We had examined half of the lot.

"Well, what the hell do you know about that?" I said.

What Peru said cannot be printed.

These pictures, these photos, were every one of infants in swaddling clothes or out of them, male and female infants of all ages under a year.

My head felt like the foam on a glass of beer. If Mason was a blackmailer, this was certainly blackmail in a lighter vein. In a smuggled whisper I said, "My God, Peru, does Raffy expect us to pick his out of these?"

It was no joke to him. As his lips curved to snarl some answer, I saw a flash of surprise in his face, and with a twist he flung himself backward, in behind the telephone screen in the corner.

I should have snapped off the light and slid to cover under the bed. But while I still sat foolishly on the floor, the door was opened quickly and I was staring at the useful end of a small revolver.

The woman whose name I remembered, the Countess de Sieffert, Mrs. Mason's only pal, was standing in the doorway. She was in a sort of black, nun-like négligé, but her hair was still flaming in a stiff globe about her head. Her face, when I took my eyes from the barrel of the gun, was not pale, not excited.

Stiffly, for the first time in my life, I lifted my hands to the level of my shoulders, and slowly, as she motioned with the gun, I rose from the floor.

12

Secrets

"SIT DOWN—THERE," she said. "With your right hand raised, with your left hand—take off that mask. Do not hesitate."

Her voice had still that trace of accent. There was an occasional something about her sentences, too, that hinted her foreign origin. Her voice sounded as if she would not ask again.

She had everything in her favor, and it didn't suit my book to be winged there at that time. She came forward a step or two, as if perhaps to tear the mask away herself, but I saved her the trouble and pulled the cloth to one side.

I thought of Peru, that she didn't know of, there behind the screen, with his gun. He had orders not to kill Gray Mason, but none regarding anyone else!

I saw her eyes widen slightly with recognition, and she murmured, rather oddly, "Yes, you." Then sharply, "Your hands, keep them lifted." Standing about two yards away, she stared at me, perhaps trying to recall my name, since she had probably heard it at the party. She seemed in no hurry.

"You are—Mr. Peters of the other night!" said the Countess triumphantly, as if she was pleased to remember my name. "So!" (She pronounced it "Soh!") "Mr. Peters, Mr. Mason's guest, a second-story person!"

"No, Countess," I answered, "you have me wrong. I merely dropped in to pay a visit and found Mr. Mason away from home. I'm a particular friend of his, you know, and he has asked me to make free in his home at any and all hours. Now, Countess, don't fire that gun of yours and don't get nervous. You see I'm keeping my hands up. I think I'll run along if you don't mind. Look, I'm turning my back—"

While I kept up this stream of talk, my hands on high, I rose little by little from the chair and moved toward the hall door, deliberately giving her my back for a good broad target. If Peru got my idea, it would be best for all concerned.

He did all right. The screen was three big steps behind her. When she turned away from it, he had his chance, and out he came with a stealthy rush.

I glanced around in time to see the end of it. He came toward her with arms outstretched, intending to stop her mouth with one hand and get a tight hold on her body. In ten silent seconds he would have had her helpless.

But the babies, the little innocent babies were his undoing. His foot slipped on some of the strewn photos. He lunged downward unintentionally and his next two steps brought him close to the floor. His shoulder took the Countess in the knees, and down they went together.

But she had heard the foot that slipped, and had a split second to turn in. She saw Peru tottering toward her. No sound came from her lips, but as they reached the floor together her revolver came down with concentrated force, striking Peru solidly on the side of the forehead.

The gun had bounced on the floor, just out of reach of the Countess, at my feet. It was a wonder that it hadn't exploded. I toed it under the bed.

"Countess, I'll attend to him," I said. Kneeling beside Peru, I got out the vial of the latest anaesthetic that he was carrying in his pocket. It came from Doc Clurges, one of Raffy's satellites. I administered it to Peru and soon had him totally inert, breathing heavily.

Then I turned to the Countess where she was standing calmly in the middle of the floor, staring at me. I said, "Now we can talk business. I'm glad to have that bird out of the way. Rough on you, Countess, but he had a gun, and I didn't want him to plug you."

It would not have surprised me if she had tried to get out of the room, or shouted for help. But it did not surprise me either to see her waiting there, looking at me with her round stare. In a way, her big brown eyes had a curious innocence. She looked bargainable, anyhow.

"Now, then, Countess," I said—"by the way, you're not afraid of me, are you?"

She shook her head. "Me?—I am afraid of nothing. I do not believe in fear. And of you, Mr. Peters, who could be afraid?"

"That's fine," I said. "That means there's no prejudice on either side. Now seriously, Countess, can you promise that you won't do anything to interfere with my freedom if I remain here for a few minutes longer—and don't molest you, of course?"

"But why not?" she said, with a look of wonder that had me guessing whether it was as genuine as it seemed. "I have learned that one may make strange partnerships" ("partnairships," she pronounced it) "and not be cheated. Are we not both looking for the pictures?"

"The pictures! You're looking for Mason's pictures! Well, here they are!" I pointed with my foot at the contents of the rifled safe, the baby photos spread over all that corner of the room.

"Not those, not those!" she said.

"You've seen these here?"

"No, but he would not keep the real ones there, so plain, so easy to obtain. That is for common thieves."

"I think you're right," I admitted slowly. "I assume you've checked all the obvious places; you've been in this house long enough, I know. God knows what *you* want the pictures for—I'm not trying to pry into your affairs, understand—but—"

"What are *you* here for, then?" she darted in suddenly. "Are you not trying to protect someone against a madman?"

"Madman?" I didn't comprehend. "Madman? You mean Mason?—but, Countess, what about him? Any chance he's going to interrupt us?"

"Nevair!" Impulsively she spoke aloud, then hushed her voice. "But he may be here tonight."

This time it was certainly my turn to stare at her.

"He is trying to get back, that is what I mean."

"Trying? What's going to prevent—?"

"As long as Harriet Mason lives, that man will never set foot in this house again. It is her own property. But—who are you, if you do not know this?"

"Never mind," I soothed. "Just trust me and keep on talking. It listens well. We're allies, remember."

"He tried to come in last night, but the servants would not admit him. Tonight, I think, he has bribed one who may admit him. But it is late. We must get the pictures before he comes. We waste time."

"Maybe we do," I said, "but I want a little more light on this. Tell me some more. If Mason sneaks in here I can handle him."

"If I tell you more, Mr. Peters, you will get the photographs for me?"

"I'll do my damndest, Countess, but you know how it is. I don't know where they are."

"Ah, but I know!" she said. "Only I cannot obtain them. I am not strong enough."

"You have me beat, Countess," I confessed. "If you know where the pictures are, you'd better lead me to 'em, but there's just one thing I'd like to know. I've been sent here to get a picture, and I know what picture. But that's all I do know. Suppose you tell me—what's Mason's little game?"

"Ah, that you do not know? Wait—I will show you. Oh, he will never play his game again, Mr. Peters. That woman's death in this house may have ended his power—always." A quaint speech.

"I could tell you so much about that man," she went on. "How much his wife has endured for all these years, and she so good, really so good. Ah, how she has suffered from that man, and yet she could do nothing. Because her family would not permit her to divorce him, you understand. Or even to live apart, according to the will. She would lose control of her money, and she does so much good with it."

I was listening and watching in amazement. What she did was as surprising as what she said. She had pulled out the left hand lower drawer of the table, which I knew for a fact contained nothing but blank, unused paper, and she had taken out whole reams of it, placing it on the floor. I would have told her that it was useless, but by this time I was prepared for surprises.

But I did venture a mild, "What are you looking for in there?"

"The copies of his letters. He keeps the copies always, the impression beneath, you understand. I believe that there is time."

"I've looked—"

"But surely you did not know how to look. He uses a peculiar kind of carbon paper. It is not carbon paper at all. He does not use the real. He prepares it himself in the photographic room.

"There is a green page which shows where—I shall find it soon. Oh, what a husband! These parties, these people he has brought in here, and poor Mrs. Mason I could not protest, though she knew the people they were. But now she can stand it no longer. She has broken with him at last, and it may be that the court will allow her to keep her money, which is hers. It is all hers, the house, the money, the family. But such a husband! It is what may happen if one marries an American in Europe. Ah, now I have them!"

She had separated out some pages that looked to me I perfectly untouched like the rest.

"I think I have some letters," she said. "There is an electric heater in the bathroom. Bring it here, insert the plug in the footboard, and I will show you."

Half-stupefied, I did as she ordered. The heater had a face so flat that I supposed it had been specially made, for it didn't look as if it could throw heat at a very large angle.

"To prove that he is mad, I am showing you these," said the Countess. She took from the writing table an instrument whose use had puzzled me, cushioned pincers with a long handle. The jaws closed on the paper so softly as to leave no mark, and she held the sheet a few inches from the face of the heater, allowing it to receive an even warmth.

"I watched him do this once," she said.

Gradually words formed on the page, connected lines of writing, a wide-margined letter that filled the , page and ran over on the other side. The Countess withdrew the sheet and held it out to me.

"Soh!" she remarked.

I hardly felt the warmth of the paper between my fingers while I read the message of the invisible ink. Of this letter, dated sometime in the previous year, the body ran as follows:

DEAR MRS. HONEOYE:

You will never know who I am, but I am a person of the utmost discretion. I merely write to you in order that you may be reassured that, though the little matter of the Thornton legacy is understood by me, the facts will go no further. The later, holographic will of your common law husband, Lloyd Thornton, was never found. That is, it was in your sole possession, and soon thereafter, of course, it was impossible for anyone else to find it, as you destroyed it!

Why not, Mrs. Honeoye? The beggarly fraction of a million dollars which you have obtained from Mr.

Thornton's estate will be better used in placing a stained glass window in Plattsburg's Pro-Cathedral, than in paying old debts and feeding hungry children. However you would hardly be eager to have it known that you destroyed your elderly husband's attempt to right the wrong he did. It would add little to the beauty of the Pro-Cathedral window.

If you feel incredulous that proof of your act exists, permit me to explain that I have made a clear photographic copy of the will, easily legible. In one corner of it there is a very distinct thumb-print—yours. At the top there are several finger-prints—yours and Mr. Thornton's. No other finger-prints are visible. This is ironclad evidence that Mr. Thornton was not delirious during his last illness when he said that he had made a new will and delivered it to you.

I have said that you will never know who I am. But human designs are imperfect, and it is conceivable that you may discover my identity. It is well, then, that you should know the only contingency in which the facts will be disclosed. In the event of my death such disclosure cannot fail to take place within three months. I have arranged with the officials of a certain trust company, in whose vaults copies of my records are kept, for the evidence and full explanation to be delivered to one of our more enterprising tabloid newspapers, which will place a proper value on the material. I deplore the sensational methods of these newspapers more than I can say, but in some cases they prove useful. They are especially suitable for the reproduction of *photographic evidence.*

With all best wishes, I beg to remain
                              Sincerely yours,
                              A Trustworthy Friend.

After a little I said, "But, Countess, this is blackmail."

"No, no!" she denied, gazing at another page now toasting before the heater.

"What else can you call it, then?"

"It is not for money, you understand. He does not demand anything. I have read many of these, and destroyed them, but he never says a word of money. It is secrets, secrets, secrets—he looks for them everywhere. Then he takes pictures; it is the photographic evidence he obtains.

It is amazing, where he has gone to obtain pictures. Then he writes letters, and sends the pictures. This is his method, you understand."

Yes, I was beginning to understand in full the hobby of Gray Mason. Yes, and beginning to wonder—

But a little cry of surprise from the Countess diverted my thought. She had begun to put the blank paper back in the drawer. Now she held up a page thickly typed on both sides. She waved it, displayed it with a childish excitement.

"A letter he had not sent!" she cried under her breath. "It lay beneath the paper. Look, it is the Brovard letter, not copied yet. It is addressed to her. Now we shall know why that poor woman died."

"If it tells that it will be a wonder," I declared. "Of all the incompre—by jingo, Teddy Brovard may quit faking insanity now!"

It was a draft letter with a few longhand alterations.

My dear Miss Brovard:

You must pardon me for addressing you properly as "Miss."

You will never know who I am. Sufficient to say that we both owe a great deal to our host, Mr. Mason, you for his charming hospitality to you and your brother and his generous assistance in helping you to avoid the clamorous public, I for his unintentional disclosure of your fascinating history, including the real motive for the murder of your victim, Mr. Abe Johnson, and the unique method of procedure adopted by you and your aforesaid brother in this crime.

Mr. Mason's selection of "Passion's Golden Dye" to exhibit at the reception in your honor proves his simplicity. If he had made one or two obvious inferences from that narrative, he must have realized that the Johnson murder as it was detailed in court and the Johnson murder as it actually occurred were unlike as black and white. I may add that certain studies I have made in the genealogy of your family have revealed the fact that your lover and victim, Mr. Abe Johnson, was until his unfortunate demise the first in line of succession to the half-million dollars which will be left by the aged Cyrus P. Turner, originator of the tree-transplanting business. Strange to say, this fact was not known to Mr. Johnson, who had not the genealogical acumen of you and your—brother.

It naturally strikes the observant mind that so astute and painstaking a planner as yourself, my dear Miss Brovard (for to you must go the chief credit for the plot in all its subtlety), after getting rid of one of the two lives between you and the Upton fortune, may imitate the ambitious heroine of "Passion's Golden Dye" and remove the second life also, namely that of the gentleman passing for your husband, actually your brother. Possibly by this time he is wondering too.

Finally dear Miss Brovard, let me congratulate you on what seems a truly new turn in the art of murder. Finding whose life stood in your way, you bravely determined to take that life without concealment, knowing that in this enlightened country such an act would possibly result in your having to stand trial and be acquitted. You merely concealed your true motive, gain. I congratulate you, and I assure you that though I share your secret, it shall go no farther. You cannot, of course, be brought to trial again for your first murder, no matter what new facts come to light about you, but in any case I am only too anxious to observe your future tactics, and should not dream of doing anything to divert you from the problem: How to dispose, with no risk, of the second life, your brother's.

My kindest regards to your brother, and believe me

Yours sincerely,
An Ardent Admirer.

It certainly cleared up the Brovard affair. For Teddy Brovard had known! And being a blunt, downright sort of fellow without much brains, but with a strong desire to have his own way, he had taken his own way with Madeleine.

I glanced at a small jade clock standing on the dresser, still ticking. It said a quarter to four.

"It's almost morning. Do you suppose—?"

She said, "He will come. I know now he will come for the letter. He cannot leave it. Do you not see?—he was so carefully watched that night that he could not destroy it when the woman was dead. The police watched, I watched, Mrs. Mason watched, and he could do nothing with this letter he had written to the dead woman. A servant was with him when he packed—"

"What!"

"She *drove* him out of the house!"

My idea was growing on me; the guess I made before I read the Brovard letter had become a moral certainty. Now I knew why in all my wanderings about the dives and docks, in all my loitering in the streets at night and listening to the talk of the down-and-outs, I had never heard a word of Clever Julian, the dining-out thief and blackmailer. Doubly clever, the clever one had disappeared, not down among the dregs, but up among the lofty. By the luck of the clever, he had wooed and won a Fortune, after borrowing himself a Name.

And then—! Why had I been so dense so long? It was obvious now. The clever one was constrained. He was no longer the keen Raffles, the sportsman, who throve on the knowledge of his own cleverness. He could not tamper with locks of doors and jewel-boxes any longer; huge wealth had taken the salt away from all that.

But he could steal secrets! Cunningly, patiently, he could worm out secrets, an artist for art's sake. And in stealing secrets he had gone mad!

13

The End of Clever Julian

AND MRS. MASON—"Tell me about Mrs. Mason," I said. "Does she know—how much does she know?"

"Not one half, not one tenth, or she would have died—or killed him!"

"Then tonight—she doesn't know that you are here, searching—?"

"Surely not! I do everything for her, and for someone else."

I considered for just a moment. "Hm! Jul—Mason must have been pretty bad, if she couldn't stand him even without knowing about this Family Skeleton Department of his."

"She suffered—how she has suffered! I can't tell you. This last party, this woman's death, they have nearly killed her."

"Well, I'm for her, Countess. I'd like to see Mr. Gray Mason squashed under somebody's thumb. But there are two things I want from him first, a picture and the answer to a question. I want 'em both bad."

"I will help you get the picture," she said quickly. "We can destroy all the pictures now, if you will open the hiding-place."

"And where is that?" I demanded, with a sudden awakening to the fact that we had spent many minutes beating about the bush without getting at the business in hand.

She pointed to the low, broad radiator beneath the space where the safe had been. "In there, at the end away from the pipe."

I gave her an incredulous look. "In there! But, Countess, they'd be ruined in a week when the heat's turned on."

"The three last sections do not receive any steam and the pictures are in the last. Look for yourself to see."

I got down to it and examined the segments carefully. Without doubt some amateur plumbing had been done at the junction of the third and fourth segments. Perhaps the opening had been shut. I rapped the sections with my knuckles, however, and all of them sounded hollow.

"What makes you believe that the pictures are in there?" I asked.

"Because I have seen him put them there. I watched from the dark room last week. There is a tube he puts them in first."

"Very well then, Countess, there's just one good course to follow tonight. We will let Gray Mason open the hiding-place for us, and then we'll do what we like with the contents."

"But the question you are going to ask?"

"He will answer it if my hands are at his throat!"

"You mean—wait for him to come? Suppose he does not!"

"You have said he will. I think it's certain that he will, if only to get the Brovard letter. If he doesn't open up the hiding-place of his own free will we can find ways to persuade him!"

"You are very fierce, Mr. Peters!"

"But I am right, Countess."

I examined Peru, who seemed to be in a state of slumber, though he stirred a little. I took his gun and put it in my hip pocket, and dragged him into the bathroom. I took possession of the Countess's little gun also, where it lay beneath the bed. She was gathering together the baby pictures and stuffing them in the safe. I helped, and when they were all inside, closed the safe, and with some assistance from her, got it into the dark room. Peru's tools, and all other signs of visitation were concealed. The picture hung straight in front of the forced door where the safe had been. Superficially, the room showed no sign that three persons had been marauding there.

"I'll allow him an hour," I said, when our vigil had begun.

"He is very late," said the Countess from where she was sitting on the bed. "At first I thought you were he. But I saw you—"

"D'you want your gun back, Countess?"

"No. You may keep it for the present." We waited. Time went by. I broke the silence. "A car has just stopped outside the house, Countess. It may be Mason's. If it is, let me tackle him alone. I'll choose my time. You get me, don't you?"

"Oh, yes, Mr. Peters, I will do as you say."

I was at the corridor door, listening. "You don't mind waiting in there in the dark room?"

"I will not mind."

"I think he's coming," I whispered close to her ear. "Any minute now." With Peru's flash I lit the carpet for her feet to reach the dark room entrance beyond the bed. She disappeared inside and that door closed quietly.

I slipped into the clothes-closet, and waited there with my hand on the door knob, already turned so as to preserve quiet when opening.

Mason must have come rapidly upstairs. He almost burst into the room. I pushed my door open an inch and kept my eye to the opening.

The corner light snapped on, and I saw Mason, apparently in dinner dress, standing on the radiator, his back toward me.

I got a surprise. "He put one over on you, Countess," I thought. "The safe was just a blind for ordinary thieves like me, but the radiator was a blind for cleverer folks like you. Whatever's in the radiator, it's not the precious pictures."

Gray Mason was standing on the radiator, but not in order to examine the safe or its contents. Instead, he had done something to the broad, thick, gilded frame of the painting that hung there, causing one entire side of it to bend downward like an arm. Out of the thickness of the inner side of the arm he nudged with his little finger what looked like a slender packet. He then lifted the arm and settled it into place, so that the carved work concealed the join. He descended from the radiator and turned his attention to the writing table. He opened the left hand lower drawer and looked inside and pushed it shut again. He had seen that it had been disturbed. I saw his shadowed face for a moment as he stared quickly into the corners of the room as if he suspected watchers; there was fear in his eyes. His arm shook as he reached to put out the light.

With my finger ready on the button of the flashlight, I advanced to meet him, but he collided with some one else instead! There was a burst of light as my finger involuntarily pressed the button, and I stumbled and almost fell. Mason gasped; I believe he was voiceless with fright at the sounds in the darkness. I reeled in his path, and he reeled too. I felt his hands pushing me off—I heard something fall on the floor—I saw the packet bounce and disappear from the lighted zone. Then the light went out—that five seconds was more confused than even my telling of it—and I knew somehow that Mason was in the hall, fleeing.

Clever Julian was in the hall, escaping! The man who knew the answer to the question I had to ask! That was all I had brain for, that and the fact that this blundering, stamping creature in the darkness was Peru, and that I had to see him out of the house. I got him by the scruff and into the corridor. I scuffled him along to the stairs and down, not half a minute behind Gray Mason himself.

The door into the street stood open, as Mason had left it, and I dragged Peru out. There was the faintest trace of daybreak.

One of the lanterns set in the middle of the street was still standing there; the other, the arc-light revealed, was overturned, smashed. The street seemed empty. I looked about helplessly, holding up Peru.

From the darkness of the sheds across the way a motor sprang into life, a taxicab emerged from the shadows with almost a leap. "Hop in," came the growled command. "What youse been doing, movin' the piana?"

This was the cab that had been waiting for us since a quarter to three. I shoved Peru in and clambered in myself. "Where is he?" I asked wildly. "He had a car, didn't he?"

"The little guy? Sure, a big Arrow. I come up because I seen him stop here."

"Follow him—quick!" I gasped. "Can you catch him?"

"A cinch. I could catch that guy if he was in a plane. He knocked over one of them lanterns gettin' out of here."

I leaned back in the seat, suddenly exhausted. My head swam. Peru slumped into the bottom of the cab.

We had swerved and gone down the Avenue at fifty. Ten blocks ahead a solitary car showed a tail-light.

Mason must have known that he was being followed, and the knowledge apparently put the fear of God or the devil into him. Perhaps he was keyed up with liquor. He might even have been drugged with cocaine. The big Pierce spurted when we were but two blocks away; yet it hardly gained on us, so powerful an engine was concealed beneath the taxi hood. Then Mason commenced twisting and doubling, making a turn at every corner, hoping to get out of sight. But the cab was better at that game than the heavier car.

I was beginning to wonder how much longer this chase would go on without the police joining in. It was lighter now, and Mason, somewhere about Fiftieth Street and Lexington Avenue, turned east.

Perhaps in that last minute he actually went mad, stark, staring mad. Down the sloping street he went, reckless and wild, the big car swaying dangerously from side to side. Just a few hundred feet ahead of him was a short, broad, open pier, and then the East River.

I don't know precisely how he lost control of the Pierce. An early morning sprinkler had left the surface of First Avenue and the stretch to the pier extremely slippery. A leaky tire may have made the heavy car unmanageable at that speed. Whatever the cause the Pierce made two excursions onto the sidewalk in the last block, upset ash-cans, skidded first on one side and then on the other, missed a hydrant by six inches, and rolled out upon the pier.

There was a bright light there, owing to some storage warehouses nearby. Our cab was still midway in the block behind when we saw the huge car, still doing about forty, crash into the mooring block, leap sidewise, hit the guard-plank at the edge of the pier, and keel over the edge, falling upside down into the water.

Ten seconds later I was at the edge, looking over. The water was very dark.

I got in the cab again. "Scram like hell," I said.

14

Middlehaven: The Big House in the Woods

NO READER OF THIS will suppose I am a churchgoer, but it was in a church that I found the key at last to the "Pat" and "Dubrosky" letters. And it happened on the day after housebreaking, Sunday.

That morning, with alarm set for six, I was fighting yawns while I dressed. Of rest and refreshment I took but the minimum, for I thought my first duty to myself was to break camp and find a new and very secret location. Gray Mason dead—the last thing Raffy wanted—and the coveted pictures God knew where—perhaps in the possession of the Countess de Sieffert. That was a set of circumstances that admitted no excuse in Raffy's grim code. Health and happiness required that Terry Fultz remove to fresh woods and pastures new.

But the white-hot iron that burned my vitals was the loss of Clever Julian. At one seven-league step I had come so much farther than Holborn, had met and cultivated the one man, apparently, who held the key. I might have had the key had I asked one simple question, had I even let drop a casual phrase. But Fate's fashioning! When I knew who he was, he was already escaping me toward Death.

The phone rang, and though I automatically reached out my hand, I drew it back, wondering. I didn't like it, at six-fifteen a.m. on Sunday morning. But then, I thought, this is my farewell appearance, and if this means bad news, I'd better know it. I lifted the receiver and just waited.

What I heard at first was irregular breathing, then Josephine's voice: "Is he there, operator?"

I cut in. "Yes, want me?"

"Terry!" Her voice was dragging in the gutter. It had a hungry animal quality. Of course I couldn't help what name she called me by, though the settlement operator, who I didn't doubt was listening with gusto, did not know me as Terry Fultz.

"Yes, Josephine? Kind of early, isn't it?"

"Terry, listen! Peru's told him something. He's out for you. And he knows I've been seeing you."

"Aren't you just a little excited?"

"He knows I've been seeing you, I tell you."

Not the fact but the statement surprised me. "You mean those times—when Linna couldn't come—you weren't supposed—"

"No, no, my God, he wouldn't let me see anyone else. He didn't know."

"Well, of all the—"

"Stemholzer, too. He's got it in for him, Terry."

"Remember, you're on the phone."

"Look, Terry, I'll tell you when I see you. Just once, Terry. Couldn't we? I know where—"

"Oh, no, Josephine, you've told me *quite* clearly. Better save your own skin, my lovely."

"But, Terry."

"I'm leaving town, dear. Your call has just made it that much more urgent."

"But—"

"And maybe this call is a little indiscreet. Watch yourself."

A moment's pause, a heavy breath. "I hope he puts a knife into you, you—"

I never learned what I was.

I was downstairs with my big suitcase before the regular desk attendant had made her appearance; so I didn't have to enter into any long-winded explanations. I just remarked that I felt like a vacation out of town, and would send word about my trunk and mail.

In case Raffy had already sicced any of his snoopers on my trail, I cut across town on the trolley to the Christopher Street Ferry and checked my suitcase there. I intended to reclaim it after finding a place to live uptown, but I would make a bluff of starting on a journey across the ferry when I did.

I walked back and took the subway to Ninety-sixth Street. For an hour I walked around, searching for signs stuck in the window and sometimes looking at the rooms themselves. I found none that quite suited me. A back exit was an essential. Then remembering I'd had no breakfast, I dropped into the first eating place and ordered ham and eggs.

A *Times* lay on the seat beside me and I picked it up, wondering what might be new in any of the lines I had been concerned with. It happened to be Saturday's paper, folded with the Religious Services outermost, and I glanced it over carelessly. I had no idea of attending a service.

Something caught my eye, though, that made me stare and look again, with my thoughts flying wildly. Under the heading "Spiritualist" was the notice:

LITTLE HEMLOCK SPIRITUALIST CHURCH
100½ West End Avenue
Reverend F. Audrie Chester will speak on
"Justification of The Love Life of Dr. Kane"
10.30 A.M.
Flower Service, Spirit Messages, 8.15 P.M.

"The Love Life of Dr. Kane"—I had certainly run across something like that not so long ago. Where? I had it in a moment, the lines of Dubrosky's poem, that had made no sense to me. It was about Sister Fox and some kind of physical knocks, leading up to The Love Life of Somebody Kane. There could hardly be two Dr. Kanes whose love lives were on record. I went almost on the double back to the subway and rode downtown to Sheridan Square, for the copy of the poem was in my suitcase. There was time for me to recover the case and get up to West End Avenue before the Reverend Chester had finished speaking. I'd nail him afterward and find out things. If he could give a meaning to the Love Life he could probably explain the whole poem.

So I took my case out of the check-room temporarily and right there in the waiting room I read the poem over again. It seemed just as incomprehensible as ever to me.

LINES ON MORAL NECESSITY

An object more completely ramshackle
Than Bethel's former princely tabernacle
I can't imagine to exist.
Even a glum evangelist
Who beats his drum and swings his scourge
And rivals Jeremiah's dirge
Admits the edifice is crumbling,

Or else he'd have no 'scuse for grumbling.

A person of intelligence
Sees morals gently going hence,
And no amount of foam and lather,
No quantity of fuss and blather
Will keep an impious generation
From blithely moving toward tarnation.
One does not need go very far
To see how brief religions are.
Of revelations near this shore
There have been many—I pick four.

Jemima, Universal Friend,
On whom the Godhead did descend,
Who lived across from Louis P.
Before a king he came to be,
Her stock of miracles extended
A pious race (alas, 'tis ended)
To wear strange dress and stranger doctrine.
Where were their wits, they never locked her in?

The lowly cot where Sister Fox
Obtained the hyperphysical knocks
Availed not Margaret to know
That future years would bring her woe.
Or that in covers green in vain
The Love Life of Elisha Kane
Would seek to clinch her claim to pelf
His family would not pay herself.

Let us not slight good Father Miller
Than whom no prophet was an iller;
For when he had, I understand,
Obtained his people's goods and land,
He told them where to meet their doom,
And there was hardly standing room.
Assembled, chanting, for their Fate
They waited long. They still await.

Let's turn our eyes another way
And meditate on Joseph's clay.
The tablet carried in his hat

Contained a revelation that
When published filled the world with jeers
That warbled sweet in Joseph's ears.
The holy hill, the sacred grove
Remain, but all the plural drove
Left the fat land in western flight,
To settle on a desert site.

The lesson that I draw from these
Is: Revelation, on its knees,
Beseeches us not to forget it,
And save our souls—and yet—and yet it
Seems that those who live to flout it
Are just as cheerful when without it
As for what happens after death—
I've not died yet, and save my breath.
And hence no one with common sense
Will venerate the commandments.

I found the church, a quaint little building of stone made
to imitate wood, between two enormous apartment houses.
I stood along with a lot of others, and didn't know much
more about the subject when the Reverend Mr. Chester had
finished. He was a rather puny, elderly man. but he had
energy and a fine shrill voice that sawed your nerves up. He
was so excited that his words ran together, and not being
there for the whole talk, I didn't get much out of the last ten
minutes of it. Only this:

There had been a real Doctor Kane, and he had married
Margaret Fox, and there were no two ways about it. Anyone
who said he hadn't was a so-and-so. The Love Life seemed
to be a book on the subject written by Margaret herself. It
all must have happened quite a while ago.

He ended quicker than I had expected, and turned and
walked toward a small green door in the corner behind the
throne. I was after him, and I pushed on when he tried to
shut the door after him. We were in a robing room, by the
colored garments hanging on the wall.

"Excuse me, Mr. Chester, for intruding like this. I haven't
been here before, but I've got something mighty important—"

"I cannot hear you before the Morning Messages," he
snapped. "The service is not finished."

"I'm awfully sorry. I'd cheerfully give a hundred dollars for a little information from you, Mr. Chester, but I'll have to wait, I guess."

"What's that?" he asked sharply.

"I said it was worth a hundred dollars to me to have you tell me something."

"Ah! Then perhaps—" he was struggling with a crimson robe which felt velvety when I helped him wrap it around him—"thank you. I shall not detain you long. I mean it will not take long."

"I'll wait with pleasure," I told him, and he departed into the big hall again. He was back again much sooner than I had expected, locking the door behind him. He had a weary look, and touched his hand to his forehead.

"Too much resistance," he murmured. "The messages would not come through."

That was very lucky for me, of course. He slung off his robe and sat in a chair. "What is it, Mr.—?"

"Adamson," I said. "Arthur Adamson. Kindly read this." I thrust the poem in his face.

He took it and read it—at least he read it part way through. At first he was puzzled, then his face grew red. He crumpled the poem in his fist and glared up at me, and I knew he had hit Margaret and the Love Life.

"This is outrageous, sir!" he barked in that shrill voice of his, "This lying—er—doggerel—"

It looked as if he was going to tear the poem up and trample on it, but I grabbed it. I assured him that I hadn't written the poem, that I didn't know who had, that I didn't understand who were the people referred to, and that if I did understand I'd think as badly of the writer as he did.

"I see—I see," he murmured, leaning back with a faint sneer. "Blasphemy—lies—derision."

"You must be right," I admitted. "But I'd like it explained."

"What can need explanation?" he asked.

"Everything," I said. "Who are all these people mentioned by their first names that you seem to recognize? And what's more, where are they? And what's more, if you can tell, where was the writer of the poem when he wrote it?"

"It should be obvious, Mr. Adamson, that the names are those of modern prophets who brought spiritual revelation in the last century in the lands of this state."

My blood was jumping. "The lands of this state! Go on, Mr. Chester, go on!" I cried. "You've got just what I want."

Then I learned all about it. Jemima was Jemima Wilkinson, who worked miracles; the Fox sisters were Kate and Margaret, who had begun receiving spirit messages in a big way. Doctor Elisha Kent Kane was a famous (but not to me) Arctic explorer who had married Margaret, without a clergyman. Father Miller was the man who discovered that the world would come to an end in 1844. Joseph was Joseph Smith, founder of Mormonism. And all these people had flourished before 1850 in a portion of Western New York you could walk over in a day, between Rochester and the Finger Lakes.

"Revelations near this shore," the poem said. That might mean the shore of one of the Finger Lakes or of Lake Ontario. I showed him the letters I had brought along containing the various names, but he knew none of them.

I pumped his arm. "Thank you, sir, a thousand times!" I took out my pocketbook and extracted one of the two hundreds it contained.

But he waved it away. "I couldn't, I assure you," he said faintly, adding as I evinced surprise, "but there is an Offering Box beside the entrance!"

"My mistake," I said. "Thanks again."

Out in the street I could have kicked my heels with glee. I was so crazy that I hopped right into the nearest booth and got Information at Grand Central. I learned that by speeding I could get to the station and catch the Cayuga, which would land me in Rochester before ten that night.

I did catch it, and had time to buy a big automobile map of the country I was going to.

Between Charlotte, the port of Rochester, and Oswego there seemed to be three or four small bays or river-mouths with communities attached. They were probably resorty places with a skeleton population in winter. That wouldn't necessarily be out of keeping with the letters, since there might be a few big houses nearby where the well-to-do lived the winter through.

I asked the conductor what about getting to one of them that night. He said there was no train connection with the Cayuga for any of them, wouldn't be for another month. No bus connection either, except for one, Middlehaven.

"What is it like?"

"Small place. Built up mostly in the last few years. Not much beach. Probably pretty dead right now."

It was ninety per cent darkness when I alighted at Newark, N. Y., for Middlehaven. A moon, however, was due in about half an hour. A muddy old bus driven by a shoddy old driver took me slowly northward over a road of ruts and holes, a long fifteen miles.

I remember coming to suddenly and learning it was time to alight. Then I heard the water moving beneath the wind. I remember fighting the wind off the lake, stumbling along an ill lit and deserted street, and finding my way eventually into a place where a long counter filled one side of the room and an aproned barkeep passed drinks out to roughly dressed men.

I got into conversation with one of these men, a lank, hesitant-mannered chap with a bald spot, one Jobson.

"Your line of work, Mr. Jobson?" I asked.

"I run a small nursery, sir." And, I apparently staring, he explained, "A plant nursery, sir, for the summer folks."

"And in the winter?"

"I keep a boat, sir, and I sneak up on some unsuspecting whitefish an' sturgeon—at all proper times and seasons, sir."

"And where, Mr. Jobson, might I find a place to stop in Middlehaven for more or less of a visit?"

"Well, the place isn't on its feet for the season altogether yet. Why not with me, sir? I takes in a few parties and gives 'em their breakfusts. You can git your other meals at Mooney's."

"Splendid!" I said, and we shook hands on it.

"And may I inquire, sir, what you may be doing in Middlehaven village?" he asked after another drink. "No impoliteness meant."

"None taken," I answered, "I don't mind your asking in the least, Jobson, for I'm here to tell people what I'm here for and to see if they can help me find it."

"Oh, yes, sir?"

"I'm here to look for a person who must have lived in these parts some years ago."

"What name, sir?" he asked, as we went into our third drink.

"What name? I can't tell you, man." I gave a contemptuous laugh. "D'you suppose if I knew her name I'd be
obliged to—"

I lifted my glass, and Jobson said, "Of course not, sir.
Only, when you're usually looking for a person, you knows
their name."

"Well, I don't, I tell you," I insisted. "The only name I ever
heard of anyone giving her was no name at all—just a joke.
Philadelphia Boston! What do you think of that? Who'd ever
have thought up a name like that?"

Jobson's bald spot underwent a transformation as I spoke.
It quite glistened with surprise, and his face matched it.

"Philadelphia Boston, sir? That's not a joke, sir. That *is* a
name, a real young lady's name!"

"What!" I shouted. "Philadelphia Boston's a name—an
honest-to-God name! You know it?"

"That was old Mr. Boston's queerness," said Jobson.
"Before he made his money he was in one of those sects,
you know, sir. Common hereabouts. Christadelphians, they
called themselves, and he would have the girl named
Philadelphia."

My head was whirling. All the trouble and turmoil I'd have
escaped if I had known a real name when I saw it! I wanted
to ask a hundred questions at once, and I wanted to act.

Then came a diversion. At one end of the bar a big, hairy,
red-gold man was leaning with a crowd of admirers about
him. I had noticed him unbuttoning his tongue when I came
in, sprawling carelessly with his arms spread along the bar,
conscious of his superiority. From time to time in my remarks with Jobson I had heard his big, roaring voice telling
some tale or other, and sometimes came a chorus of ap-
proval.

Now suddenly he was standing before me, with hungry
blue eyes and the red bristling beard without a white hair in
it, though the lines of his forehead showed a man of sixty or
upwards.

He boomed, "You asked Mr. Jobson about the Bostons?"

"Yes, I did. I suppose the Boston place is near here?"

"Oh, aye," he answered. "Old Boston built his mansion
over at Two-mile in the woods beyond the ponds.
Fifty-thousand House, they called it because he sank that
much in it, a tidy sum in those days. I take it you're a
stranger hereabouts?"

"I am a stranger, but I'm mighty anxious to get to that house," I said. "Is it within walking distance?"

"Why, yes, in a manner of speaking, within walking distance."

Some of the man's admirers offered to laugh at this, thinking it might be humorous. He turned his neck, and the laugh subsided.

"Then I'm going there!" I declared. "As sure as I stand here, Mr. Jobson, I'm going there tonight. If you'll carry my case to your place when you're ready, I'll go to the Boston house right now. I'm going to see it tonight; nothing else will satisfy me."

There was a murmur from those listening, and Jobson had started an "Oh, no," when he caught the eye of Red Beard and desisted.

"I'll give you your directions," said Red Beard. "Come outside and I'll point you out the way."

"I'll have one more drink," I said. "Any and all, name your choice."

Red Beard stood with his arms akimbo watching me while I took down my fourth or fifth, and then he guided me toward the door.

"My suitcase, Jobson?" I called from the entrance.

"I'll take it home, sir," he said in a curious voice, which I didn't notice then in my furious eagerness. "Mine's the second from the turn, right hand side, with the ground in front of it."

Outside, Red Beard led me until I could see a road sloping over a hill, with a string of feeble street lights extending half way up. He told me my course from there.

Somewhere I lost my path, for I have a distinct recollection of playing hide and seek with the distant green eye of a railway signal that kept appearing and disappearing. Eventually, getting weary, I cut away from the tracks, lured by what seemed to be the distant glint of water. I got to the water across a manured field and found it was what I had been looking for: the ponds.

The woods were nearer now. As the road continued toward the trees, I kept to it, and I noticed with surprise that it seemed to have been more used once than now. Now only a cart track, it had formerly been amply wide enough to permit traffic both ways.

Red Beard had declared that the place was not more than half a mile inside the woods, and I thought I had gone all of that, without seeing a sign of it. Retired from the road, he had said, but if retired it must have a private way debouching somewhere on the road. I went further and still saw no sign of it.

I commenced to retrace my steps, peering on both sides of the road. Presently I found what I wanted, and my ears were startled to hear the cry that came from my lips. There was, on the south side of this road which paralleled the shore, the entrance to a driveway.

But such an entrance for Fifty-thousand House! The wooden gateposts were long unpainted, and one of them had fallen on its side. The gate itself lay flat, and it was impossible that anything could have passed that way for a long, long time, perhaps not for all the years since Pat had written her last letter to Dubrosky.

I walked over the prostrate gate and on along the drive. At this particular point, as it happened, the trees and undergrowth were thicker than at any part of the woods I had seen. Only a little moonlight flickered through. But suddenly I came to a clearing, or at least to a place denuded of the taller trees. I could see the moon and stars above and the encircling belt of woodland beyond. But there was no house there.

I stared and stared, and uttered another cry.

There was no house there. But the side of a house was standing with its edge toward me. As I moved to one side I saw its hollow window-casements.

Then I knew why the woodland I had passed through was thinned almost throughout. Fire long ago had destroyed all but the one wall of the big house in the woods.

15

Middlehaven: Jobson's Nursery

I GOT BACK to Middlehaven that night, but I don't remember much about it, except that by instinct I went to the shore and followed its ups and downs eastward toward the village. The street lights had been turned off, but I still had the moon for a lantern, and I found Jobson's place and staggered wearily in. A feeble electric bulb in the hall showed a message tacked to the plaster. Jobson had left me directions for reaching my room.

I woke up with a slight head on, stretched across the bed half-dressed, the sun well up in the morning sky. The room had a greenwashed wall, an un-carpeted floor, and a grayish tendency in the cottony bedsheets. The furnishings were of a happy-go-lucky description and included a washstand consisting of a chest of drawers whose handles were missing and a rocking chair with one rocker curling under on which I would certainly never trust my weight. My landlord had neglected to leave a mirror anywhere in the room; so I decided not to shave.

Jobson had "ground" in front of his house, and from the window I now discovered that he had more in the rear. He was digging in it. He seemed to have a substantial nursery, which contained a greenhouse fifty feet long and a number of cold frames. There were hardier plants exposed to the weather, bulbs shooting, a few flowers actually in bloom, and whatnot.

I thought of the red-bearded man who had sent me goosechasing, and of Jobson and the others who had let him do it, but I wasn't sore. They had just plunged me into the cold water that I was bound to encounter later. I went down to see Jobson and found him looking mournfully at a bed of lily-like, drooping yellow flowers with purple-tinged petals.

"What's the matter with them?" I asked, coming up to him suddenly.

He gave a start and looked at me with his mild, nervous face. "They got coaxed out too soon, sir, these here adder's tongue. We've had more than our share of heat this spring. They ain't a-going to last another frost."

"Oh, no?" I asked. "Nice fresh morning, Jobson."

"Yes, 'tis, sir." I saw him looking doubtfully at me out of the corners of his eyes, "Ready for breakfast?"

"You might think so, after my walk last night, but I've got a bit of a head. I'd rather try a bromo."

At the mention of the walk I could almost see the beadlets break out on Jobson's brow. He raised his neckerchief and dabbed. "Now, I hope that you're not a-goin' to hold last night's little—" he swallowed—"joke—against us folks."

I shot the timorous nurseryman a look that made him pale, visibly pale. Then I smiled. "Not against you, Jobson. I don't hold you responsible, but I'll have a thing or two to say to that playboy with the red beard."

Jobson put his hand on my arm and looked earnestly into my face. "I wouldn't, sir, if I was you. You see how it was last night. There was the whole bar full o' men, and none of 'em would so much as dare give you a hint 't the Captin was havin' his bit of a joke with you. An' I must say, sir," added Jobson, slightly assertive, " 't you was mighty anxious to go."

"What happens when the Captain *is* crossed?" I asked. "Does a man live afterward?"

"I can't percisely say, sir. You see, I hain't never heard of any one crossin' him."

"Oh! Then I'll see what does happen. Where does he live, Jobson? I'll drop in on him right now."

The alarm in the nurseryman's face was somewhat relieved. "You can't, sir. Leastways, he doesn't live in the village."

"No?"

I then learned that the Captain—Captain Hearnshaw, perhaps a courtesy title—lived in a tumbledown shack some two miles east along the coast. That is, it had been tumbledown when he came to Middlehaven an indefinite number of years ago, but he had repaired it and made it habitable.

I found that once Jobson got going on Captain Hearnshaw he needed no encouragement. The Captain was nothing to me, of course, but given an audience Jobson cared little for that. He commenced with the first coming of the Captain to Middlehaven, which, as it antedated Jobson's own coming by an indeterminate period, was referred to as "some time back yonder."

"That's all very fascinating, Jobson," I said, in one of his pauses for breath, "and I'll listen to a load of it later. But I'm here for something else again. Suppose you ease up on the Captain for a while and give me all the news about the Boston family. Tell me all about 'em and especially where I can find 'em now."

"Lor'," said the nurseryman, "you've come to the wrong shop, sir, if you're tryin' to get the Bostons. Why, they left these parts *'way* back yonder, consider'ble before the Captin came."

"Where did they go to?"

"Can't say."

"What! A family living in an enormous place like that and lording it around here—you can't say what's become of them?"

"Wal," he answered slowly, "all I know is, old man Boston was the man who invented Piler's Cough Medicine, Good for Man, Dog an' Horse, though his name wan't anyways connected with it. He died before the place burned, an' Mrs. Boston she'd a'ready run away with some actor feller, an' Miss Philly, she'd run away too back beyond that, I'm told. The place was empty when it burned."

"Well, Jobson," I said with resignation, "I can see that unless some of the older inhabitants here are fuller of the Bostons than you, I'd better be getting out of here tonight."

He was looking over my shoulder, with a face of dismay. I turned, and there down the village street strode Captain Hearnshaw. He came along rapidly with a touch of a sailor's slouch or swing in his walk, and leaned over Jobson's newly-painted white fence.

"Jobson, come here," he said, and the nurseryman went.

So did I, and I got in the first word, though the Captain's blue eyes bored right through me. I heard Jobson gasp as I opened my lips.

"Good morning, Captain Hearnshaw," I said. "You must be quite a stranger here too. Did you know that the Boston place you sent me to last night was burned years ago?"

"By God, I'm glad to hear it!" he exclaimed, and his hairy, horny hand shot out to reach for mine as he gave a hearty laugh of appreciation. "Damn me if I thought you'd take it that way, Mr.—"

"Williamson, John Williamson," I supplied.

"Mr. Williamson." He looked straight at me, one of the most direct looks I've ever experienced. "Pleased to have your further acquaintance, sir. I'm sorry I was a little high last night."

"That's all right," I said. "I'd have gone out later to see the place. Only I warn you, I may be feeling my oats sometime myself, and then beware."

He laughed in his deep-chested way, and the red beard seemed to have a humor of its own. "That's your right, Mr. Williamson." He turned to the dumbfounded Jobson. "Morning, Jobson," he remarked. "I want some of your loam."

Jobson was more or less in a stammering state. "L-loam, did you say?"

The Captain nodded. "That's it, loam. I think yours is better than most everywhere else, and I've got to have some."

"But whatever for?"

"For my primroses, the ones I'm going to buy from you."

Jobson may have imagined that the Captain had gone mad. His jaws popped wide as an oyster shell.

"Look here, Jobson," said the Captain. "I have as much right to buy flowers from you as any of the summer folks, haven't I? You know that I have some old earth-boxes up alongside the fo'c's'le, don't you? If I take it into my head to buy a little earth and a few flowers to put into them, why am I so strange?"

"But—primroses," choked Jobson.

"You have them blooming here, haven't you?"

"Yes, Captin, those Peerlesses there, but—whatever for?"

The Captain roared at him, "For early youth and sadness—any fool knows that!"

Jobson, crushed, muttered, "Yes, Captin. Yes, Captin. Any fool knows that."

I don't know that I ever saw anything more ridiculous than Jobson's idiotic waggling head, as he yessed the Captain, who then went back to the subject of loam. "What'll you take for your most suitable loam?" he asked.

"Nothing," answered the servile Jobson. "If you want it so bad, you can have it for the taking from that corner where the Spring Snowflakes haven't sprung. But are you really going to—"

"Can nothing make you understand that I mean what I say?" demanded Hearnshaw. "I'll pay you a dollar for the use of your shovel and barrow, Jobson, and trundle it up myself."

Even I was a little stunned by this proposition, remembering how far it was up to his cabin—fo'c's'le, as he called it—on Rowell's Point. But Captain Hearnshaw took Jobson's spade out of his hand, went to the corner where the Snowflakes had failed, drawing the barrow with him, and heaped it high with a load. He then planted the shovel in the dirt, lifted the handles of the barrow, and pushed it out of the gate, along the street to where it petered out, and up the gradually rising footpath along the cliffs.

Jobson and I stared after him for a little while.

"Well," I remarked, "I suppose you might call that a sign of spring. But it must be mighty lonely up there on the headland. Maybe he wants the primroses for companionship."

Jobson gave a mighty snort. "Lonely!"

"Well, he has to find some outlet for his energies, doesn't he? He's far from a young man, but he's not ready to retire from action yet, or I miss my guess."

Jobson snorted yet louder. "Outlet for his energies!"

"Why all the fuming and frothing?" I inquired.

"He has his women, hasn't he!" declared Jobson, and went behind the house to get another spade, leaving me dumb.

It was at Mooney's that Jobson recommended me to take my meals after breakfasting at the house. I got middling-to-worse food there. I sat on the extensive covered porch, relaxed, and watched the Captain as he set out and returned from his trips that afternoon. It must have been a hard push for a man of his years, no matter how hale he was. The day darkened and the wind stiffened and the rain came in flaws, and still the Captain toiled, pushing his last barrowful, with the flowers in it, up the two-mile trail to Rowell's Point.

"He has his women, hasn't he!" Jobson would have to enlarge on that after dinner.

I ate mine at Mooney's together with Mr. and Mrs. Mooney, a pair of cottagers whose trunks and provisions hadn't come through on time, and a little, inconsequential girl the Mooneys sometimes spoke to as if she was a chattel of theirs. She slipped away from the table before the rest of us rose.

We had nothing in common to talk about except the weather, which was wrung quite dry before we got through with it. It was a thick drizzle, however, when I went out in it again, an hour later, and cut across the street in the twilight toward Jobson's. I turned up the collar of my slicker and bent my head into the rising breeze. I ran into something.

16

The Wretched Maggie

I GAVE JOBSON the shoulder. He must have been coming from the busman's garage.

"Jobson! This is a stiff wind."

"I don't know as to that, sir. We have all kinds here, blowers and whistlers and screamers and natural hell-raisers. This is somewheres between a whistler and a screamer."

"Well, let's get out of it. This rain doesn't make it any better."

But there was to be no easy chair and fireside for us within a matter of minutes.

As we came to the corner, Jobson stiffened. For there in our path, with a woebegone look on her face, the girl who had had dinner at Mooney's was standing under a maple.

"Why, Maggie," said Jobson, "what's the matter?"

She gasped, "Captain Hearnshaw, Captain Hearnshaw!"

"Well, Maggie, and what about him?" said Jobson sharply.

And so it was that I discovered that Maggie was one of the Captain's gallery of women. She told a story of going to the cabin that evening, by appointment. When she knocked, there was no answer, but through the lattice window of the fo'c's'le, as he called it, she had seen Hearnshaw "sitting at his writin'-board with his hands up to his head and his mouth wide open, starin' at me like he didn't see nothin' at all."

She was sure something had happened to him, and besought us to return with her. Jobson was incredulous, but I asked a question.

"How long did you stay there?"

"Until I got scared. I couldn't hardly get back. Oh, please come!"

Jobson and I held a consultation as privately as possible on the other side of the tree. He was disinclined to start out on a fool's errand over the fancy of a hot young woman, and in the teeth of what might turn into a good-sized pocket of rain. All the same, he'd wondered sometimes why Hearn-shaw hadn't been found with a bullet in him. "Husbands and brothers," he darkly murmured. I thought Jobson wavered between two extremes, but that the situation deserved investigation. And the three of us set out, with Jobson's lantern and my flashlight, along the rocky path. Night had descended before we had gone a quarter of the way. And the rain set in.

It had partly left off when we reached the cabin, and the clouds seemed breaking up. We could see that the place was dark, and Jobson stopped when we were still some distance away. "I don't like the look of it," he said, and Maggie let out a wail, her hundredth.

"Don't be an ass," I told them both.

As we drew near I was struck by the odd appearance of the fo'c's'le, which was so small I knew it must be a one-room affair. It was something like a pumpkin-house in a fairy-tale, and something like a miniature Swiss chalet. Its sides and back bulged a bit like the pumpkin, and it had the pumpkin-house type of stove-pipe chimney. The roof was sharply peaked like a chalet, and not a bad idea in the snowfalls I've heard about in the district. The front, facing the lake, was a straight wooden surface with broad weather-strips and had only a small door in it, off-center to the left. A big ship's lantern, unlit, hung on a nail above this door. The whole cabin seemed set some six inches above the level of the surrounding ground.

"He calls this the fo'c's'le!" I exclaimed.

"Ah, but wait," said Jobson. "Go in there and close the door behind you and you'll think you're aboard a schooner."

When we got a clear view of the door we saw it was ajar a few inches. Jobson held up his lantern and a spatter of light showed his face puckered with dismay. Then cupping his hand, as if he hailed a distant vessel, he shouted in the direction of the door. No answer came; so I stepped forward and gave the door a push. Jobson's light revealed that the place was empty of its occupant.

It was quite as Jobson had said: once you had entered and forgotten the cliffs near which the fo'c's'le stood, you might imagine yourself at sea.

There was a bare board floor we made muddy tracks on. There was one comfortable armchair, but the other chair and the table were plain deal articles, and the bed, which lay under the window opposite the latticed one, was a folding cot. I had almost expected that Captain Hearnshaw slept in a hammock. All about the walls, sure enough, were some genuine ship's furnishings, binnacle, compass, glass, and what-not, all realistically clamped tight—no chance of them tumbling in a storm! The picture-frames were screwed down, and the crockery was in racks made snug and secure. Two ship's lanterns hung beside the windows.

I said that the room looked empty, and so it was in a way, but three little fuzzy heads stared at us from the corners. "Good God, Jobson, what are those?" I asked when they caught my eye.

"The dead men, I call 'em," he said, looking at them with distaste. "Hideous little critters. They moves their knees and elbows if ye touch 'em."

I went closer to one, but didn't quite like touching it. It was a tiny man, a little heathen figure with woolly poll and bright red lips and coal-black skin that looked uncommonly real, and somehow a living expression in the eyes. The Captain might have brought it from Borneo or the Andaman Islands or one of those places you read about.

"Stuffed cannibals," said Jobson. "Take my word for it, sir. They're little to start with, you see, and then they shrinks 'em—boils 'em down."

I had heard of something like that.

A broad shelf extended around the cabin, perhaps half-way up the side. It ran right up to the door, however, and prevented it from opening more than ninety degrees. It was a useful shelf, taking the place of cupboard and sideboard and mantelpiece. It supported flowers in boxes and jars, all clamped down shipwise like the rest of the stuff on the walls. Books and papers and even a covered wastebasket were fixed there. A portion beneath the lattice window had a blotter tacked to it, and it was there that the Captain had been sitting when Maggie had been here before.

There wasn't even a chair there now, and nothing on the blotter that looked like a recent blot.

The place was cramped, and the ceiling wasn't much more than eight feet high. It was flat, yellow-painted beams and scantling. I looked up and remembered the vine-covered gable roof.

I asked, "What about the little triangle up there?"

"Nothin' there but a seaman's bag and a few odds an' ends."

Maggie wanted us to investigate that upper space, but even Jobson pooh-poohed. There was nothing for us to do but to return down the muddy cliff, none of us more puzzled than I.

The moon was looking for loopholes in the clouds, and the windy air was damp. Though the visibility was wretched, the lights of a craft were intermittently visible beyond the Point.

Jobson grumbled. "Don't make sense—him bein' out an' all. An' primroses—trundlin' loam an' primroses up the cliff!"

I wasn't so sure. Perhaps it made a kind of sense, the Captain's kind.

We left Maggie on the stoop of Mooney's.

17

The Impossible Death of Captain Hearnshaw

IT WAS MORNING, and I was again ascending the cliffs from west to east. How different now when I saw all things clear! Wonders were revealed that had been invisible in the black night. No more was Malebolge a stumbling-block. I knew what were the "strange and storied shapes along the shore." Out of Middlehaven the soil changed from sand to clay and rose into channeled cliffs that justified Malebolge, more than a hundred feet high, gigantic indentations and sculpturings. In the weathered gulf beneath the cliff big trees were uprooted and overwhelmed. Beyond the cliffs of clay the geology changed again, and there was the stone backbone of Rowell's Point.

The cabin, painted in blue-gray like the majority of the barns of this section, looked neat in the morning sun. I approached and knocked on the closed door, noticing that the lantern above was missing. Then, no answer forthcoming, I repeated Maggie's procedure of the evening before and went to the lattice window to peer in.

Once more Captain Hearnshaw was inside. But he wasn't making faces this time. There was absolutely no doubt that the man who lay on the fo'c's'le floor was dead. Men who look like that are as dead as wood.

Last night, on our entering the cabin the deal table with the lattice window beyond it had been to the right. The big armchair was beside the table near the door, and another chair stood between table and window. The cot lay beneath the other window. The fireplace with the small steersman's wheel above it faced us as we entered. Binnacle and compass were on the left of the hearth. The "stuffed cannibals" were in the corners.

The furniture was somewhat disarranged now. The armchair had been shoved into a corner and had knocked over one of the little black men, who lay-pitched under the table with his paws up. The cot had been turned on one side under the shelf on the other side of the room. So a space was left in the center, and there Captain Hearnshaw lay.

He was on his back with his head close to the hearthstone and his feet just outside the range of the door when it opened. Around him was a great puddle of water that had evidently leaked out of his blue seaman's rig and his boots and his hair. His head was twisted over on one side so that I could see his face. His eyes were closed.

I backed away from the primrose box. The Virginia Creeper climbing the trellis was an old plant, and it covered three-quarters of the casement, whose sash swung idly open. It was awkward looking in, and there were parts of the fo'c's'le you couldn't see from this window, anyhow. I thought I'd try the other. Already I had discovered that the door was locked.

As I was passing around the rear of the cabin a young man emerged from the woods. He came on rapidly, a lanky, shanky young chap in hiking costume, with a high forehead and carroty hair growing thin over the rest of his head. Within speaking distance I saw he had a little beard cropping on his chin, like red crumbs.

"Man, I'm glad to see you," he said waving his arms. "I've had a beastly night in the woods. Can I buy something to eat here?"

"I'm afraid not," I said.

"But—you live here, don't you?"

"No one lives here," I answered.

He was puzzled, and he licked his tongue around his upper lip.

"If you don't mind an impertinent question," I said, "who may you be?"

He waved, taken aback. "Good Lord, nobody. I'm a hiker."

"This isn't a very likely country for hiking," I remarked.

"That's why I chose it," he said.

"What were you going to say about last night?" I suggested.

He wasn't, of course, but my words started him. He had that queer way of waving his arms while he talked, and now he became a windmill. His information summed up to the fact that his name was Bascom Saunders, that he was a publicity man for Distal's Soap taking an early vacation, and was tramping around the country as he pleased. He had been overtaken by darkness while struggling in the heavy patch of woods running back from the shore. He finally decided to crawl under his tent and wait for morning, but the rain had soon begun to leak through and he had spent the night in misery.

"Since you've come across so readily," I said, "I'll be frank in return. My name is Williamson, and I'm staying in the village down below here, Middlehaven. I've been looking for some information, so I thought I'd come up here and see if I could get anything out of the man who occupied this cabin."

"I see," he said, evidently all at sea as to what I was driving at. Then suddenly: "But you said no one lives here."

"No one does," I answered. "Man's dead, inside there. I've just found out."

He seemed to jump. His arms and eyebrows went up, and he made a grand picture of surprise.

"Look for yourself," I said. "Try the window there behind the Creeper. That's all I've done."

He did, stiffened up when he saw the interior of the cabin. He turned to me a little shaky. "Yes, he's dead, all right. I suppose we ought to go in?"

"Try," I answered. "The door's locked."

He dashed around to the front and threw himself against the door. Though he kneed it, shouldered it, and rammed it in every way he could, it stayed put.

"What kind of a door is this, anyway?" he asked.

"It's solid pine planks nailed to crosspieces," I answered. "No panels whatever. Also, if you happened to notice when you were at the window, it has a heavy bolt thrown, and the key's in the lock inside. It may be locked as well."

I don't believe that the oddity of it struck him even then.

"Well, what are we going to do?" he said.

"You're going to do it," I answered, "because you're hungry. Go on down to the village and get help. Get your breakfast. Send up two or three men. I'll wait."

"Any particular men?"

"Yes, ask for Mr. Jobson. Tell Jobson particularly not to bring Mooney, but any other responsible people he can raise."

He started off. "But first, Mr. Saunders," I checked him, "I want you to take a look at this chimney."

We were standing a few yards away from the fo'c's'le. He looked at the chimney as I did, and we both saw a faint curl of smoke coming from the cowled pipe.

My recollection of the night before had been that there was a pile of wood in the fireplace ready to be lit.

When Bascom Saunders had disappeared, I made my way out to the cliff. I walked along the edge of the sixty-foot precipice, but came on nothing that indicated the presence of anyone the night before. There was no sign of Maggie and Jobson and me being there, even, for the surface of the cliff is mainly rubble-stone.

Rowell's Point itself noses out into the lake a little distance north of the fo'c's'le. It runs about a quarter of a mile out from the general shore line, maintains its elevation almost out to its tip, and then slants down. Beyond the tip a range of rocks extends into the lake for a hundred yards or so, so close to the mean water level that the water, even today when it was calm, covered and uncovered them.

At last I saw men approaching from the village. The newcomers were Jobson and a person who had been introduced to me yesterday afternoon as Mr. Sam Orr, retired fish-merchant and resident of Middlehaven. Bascom Saunders tagged a little way behind. It looked as if he had stopped in Middlehaven to get his breakfast but not to eat it, for he was disposing of a last sandwich when he reached the fo'c's'le half a minute later.

Jobson was agitated. "Lor' help us, Mr. Williamson, is what this young feller says true?" he asked as I met them some distance from the cabin.

I answered, "Can't be wrong, I'm sorry to say. Captain Hearnshaw's gone on his last voyage, Jobson."

"Now, I'm knocked endways to hear it," said the nurseryman in manly grief. "But how did it happen, sir?"

"That's for us to find out. It's obvious that he was out in the rain a good part of the night—the cabin's a pool—but you'll see."

Jobson shook his head sadly. "There's a great man gone, sir. I doubt we'll see his like in these parts again. By the way, sir, I picked Sam Orr 'cause he's about the solidest man in the village outside o' Mooney. Seeing that Mr. Saunders here said it might be a Coroner's case, Sam tellyphoned up to Joy where our dum Coroner lives, but his missus says he's off somewheres and maybe won't be back for a week. So Sam got the p'lice in Newark, an' the Sheriff."

"Good work," I said. "I'm glad you picked Mr. Orr. I don't doubt he'll carry as much weight as any one in Middlehaven." A glance at Sam Orr's equator assured me of this. "We want men of substance, because this is a mighty queer business."

"You don't say so," Jobson slowed up a trifle. "What d'you mean, sir?"

"Just take a look in the window," I said, "and you'll see."

"The window!" repeated Sam Orr. "Why not go in the door?"

"Because nobody's been inside the door yet this morning," I said. "It's barred, maybe locked too."

Sam Orr balanced himself on the flower box and just managed to get his chin above the window-sill. Jobson, behind him, stared in, breathing on his neck. Sam Orr gave a whoof of mortal horror at the sight of the Captain lying there stark and stiff, and when Jobson turned away after a few moments, he was pale as a pillowcase.

There was a short consultation while Saunders fumed and fretted, and we decided to try to break down the door. First two and then three of us together ran against it as hard as we could, and achieved only bruises. Then we tried smashing a heavy stone against the barrier close to the bolt. But that didn't work.

"We've *got* to get in!" cried Saunders.

"What in tunket fer?" demanded Jobson, ready to give up.

"It's obvious," said Saunders. "Supposing there was some kind of evidence in there that might be perishable. That water, for instance. It may not wait until your coroner arrives."

"But whatever fer?" asked Sam Orr. "Tain't nothin' but rainwater, is it?"

"Oh, I don't know," said the red young man. "You can't predict these things. But suppose there was poison in it, or it turned out to contain traces of Lake Ontario."

An extraordinary change came over the men from Middlehaven. Jobson fell back, open-mouthed, and Sam Orr clapped his hands over his orbit and gulped.

"Why—why—you don't mean to say you—connect that water with the Captain's death?" stammered Jobson.

"My God!" said Sam, as if he had seen a light.

"You don't mean to say—a *drownded* man is in there?" asked Jobson.

Young Saunders nodded in his red way. "I think so. But how can I know? You can see why somebody has to go inside."

Jobson appealed to me. "What do *you* think, sir?"

I nodded. "Saunders is right. It's been my opinion for some time past," I said.

"But *how—?*" cried Sam Orr suddenly, and stopped.

"That's just it," I said. "Now if this closed window shows itself to be unlatched like the other, there's a chance we can make sense of it."

No one had yet examined this window, and I had some hope of finding it unfastened. That would serve to explain some difficulties. But when Saunders had pushed and pried at the sill and sides, he said a bad word. The sash was hooked on the inside, and it had a catch that made a pen-knife useless.

"We'll have to bust the glass to do it," said Saunders.

I said, "Then I vote we try the door again. A young windfall could be handled as a ram."

The others thought this was a grand idea, and we weren't ten minutes in locating a beech whose roots hadn't gone deep enough to keep it standing in one of the "hell-raisers" Jobson had mentioned. We dragged it out to the cliff and Saunders hacked away the obstructing branches with his hatchet. Then we brought the trunk around and made ready to attack.

All four of us took firm hold, got up to a fair run, and plunged the root-end against the door. There was a crash and a splintering sound, and Sam Orr slowly crawled out from beneath the trunk, but the door didn't appear to budge.

When Jobson tried it, though, he said it gave "a mite."

"It's done it, then!" affirmed Saunders. He and Jobson and I, all there was room for, shoved against the wood, and suddenly we found ourselves looking inside, the door open as wide as it could go, on account of the shelf.

One new thing I noticed at once. The floor was covered with the marks of feet, covered. Muddy shoe-prints. They were all over the floor, in the corners, everywhere, aim- lessly. They hadn't been there when Maggie and Jobson and

I had come the night before. I knew my own boot-track, and these over-muddied ours in some cases.

The other three of us backed from the threshold, and Saunders picked out places with his toes and got to the head of the corpse. Since the fo'c's'le was really quite a small place, that would be less than ten feet or so from the door. And as I watched the red young man closely, I can vouch for everything he did.

He stooped and touched the hand that lay across the chest. "Cold," he called back to us, looking up. "Stiff as stone."

He moved over onto the hearthstone, facing us, and examined the top of the head. He looked at it carefully first, and then reached out his hand and felt a moment about the scalp.

"He's had a bump," he said. "A beastly gash here. Great guns, it looks as if the skull may have been fractured!"

"Injured before or after death?" I asked.

"Can't tell, can you? Suppose he was drowned, the blood may have washed off. There's very little blood in the hair."

He stood up where he had been squatting and stared all around. When he saw the windows he had a kind of wishful look in his eyes, and I knew why, for it was pretty clear that whoever had been there had been up to some funny business with one of them, and it was mighty tempting to examine them. But he just looked around, and the black men in the corners came in for an extra scrutiny.

"Ain't ye a-goin' to git that sample?" called Sam Orr.

"Sure thing," responded Saunders, and wrinkled his eyes for a moment. Then he took a folding drinking cup out of his outer breast pocket, the kind that has a cap. Bending beside the corpse, he set the cup on the floor and wrung the water into it from the bottom of the Captain's jacket. I was astonished at the soaked condition of the cloth.

He called attention to it. "The man was drenched," he said. Then he looked at the whole surface of the jacket and the breeches. "I won't swear to it," he remarked, "but if there aren't bits of water plants on this clothing, I miss my guess."

With the covered sample of water he turned to come out again, but at my suggestion he looked at the grate. He and I had seen a faint twirl of smoke come out the chimney two hours ago, but now the ashes were cold, wood-ashes burned down to nothing.

Saunders placed his drinking cup on the table before he rejoined us, and we closed the door. It was past noon by this time, and it was agreed that we could no nothing useful there.

Jobson volunteered to remain on the ground until the arrival of someone with official authority.

Saunders and Sam Orr were rather silent as we made our way to the village and I did nothing to keep talk alive. I knew they were puzzled, but I doubted that they were as puzzled as I was. We didn't know yet whether Captain Hearnshaw had been drowned, killed by a blow on the head, poisoned, or perhaps even shot. But it was certain, as the muddy footprints in the cabin proved, that there had been agents at work in his death, or at least others present.

But that couldn't be. For it had been amply demonstrated, and it was evident to me from the first minute I had looked through the lattice window, that whoever had been with the Captain at the time of his death *couldn't* have got out again. The windows were impassable, and the door bolted from within. It had been locked, too.

I looked at the smiling world around me, at the placid blue sweep of Ontario, at the inland billow of the new-plowed lands, and at the cheerful little village lying below us ahead, with its fresh-painted cottages all spic and span—and I wondered which was mad, the world or I.

18

A Man with Literary Tastes

YOU OFTEN hear that persons with noses flattened out at the bottom aren't as bright as they might be. The more experience I had with this kind of nose and that, in Franklin, the less I believed in this superstition of signs, the low brow and the close-set eyes and the long upper lip and all the rest. I never saw the superstition get a worse knock than in the case of the country detective who arrived from Newark that afternoon. Mr. Veen's nose might have been made of putty for all the beauty he had, but for a cute customer I've seldom seen his equal. He was educated, too, and read books.

Veen, apart from the nose that changed its intentions toward the end, was a tall, dark-skinned man with black hair and a smooth face. The moment we met he was for streaking up to the cabin. And streak we did. He didn't give a thought to the villagers in the streets or peeping out their doors. He made it clear that he didn't want to hear my story yet, and after ten minutes I was glad he didn't, as I wouldn't have had the breath. Bascom Saunders, for all he was a hiker, couldn't loaf along when walking with Inspector Veen.

The detective apologized for shutting us up. "I like to get on the scene of a case," he said, "and take in as many of the details as I can before I hear any account of it. Then I ask questions along the lines that occur to me before my mind is sullied with misconception, prejudice, and faulty observation on the part of the witnesses. Now, all I allowed the bus driver to tell me was that a murder had been committed in a cabin nearby here."

"It's not likely it is a murder, you know," I said.

"Aha," he said laying his finger against his nose and rubbing it a bit. "There you are, you see! Unjustified assumption, eh? Don't say another word!"

He pushed open the door and went straight in, and then came out again, looking black. "Why in the name of con-

juration did you allow all this cow-plash to get in here?
Who's been wallowing about?"

Saunders explained that was the condition the cabin had
been in when he entered it in the morning.

"Oh, that so?" said Veen. "Part of the case, eh?" And he
stood on the threshold with his back to us. Then he turned
to Saunders again. "I'll need a camera for this mess."

"I have one," said Saunders, pointing to his kit, which lay
over on a big stone. During the interval Jobson had collected the tent and blanket and other paraphernalia from
the woods.

Veen's eyes lighted. "Now, that's very pat," he said.
"Excellent. But you handle the camera yourself."

Saunders stood in the doorway and again beside the
Captain's body and snapped his machine at the corpse and
the footprints all over the fo'c's'le.

Then Veen went in again alone to pursue his investigation.
But this time before he examined the body he noticed a
bolt-staple lying on the floor, and that made him look closer
at the door and the lock and the bolt. Then he turned his
attention to the ceiling for quite a long while, and to the
closed trap in it, and Jobson incautiously remarked that
after coming here this morning he had wondered if after all
the body had come from up there.

Veen overheard this, being near the door, and he cocked
a sarcastic eye at the nurseryman. "So that was your idea?
A reader of Kipling, Mr. Jobson?"

"No, sir, I never did read it," he answered.

" 'The Return of Imray' came into my mind when you
spoke," said the detective. "But hardly here, but hardly
here."

He examined the door again curiously, and it was clear
that he hadn't been able to account for its condition. He
sucked his lips. "The door was open when he was found?"
he said to me at last.

"Why, no. Does it look it?"

That irritated him. "Don't question me," he snapped. "But
do you seriously mean to say that those bolts were in place
when the man was found?"

"Precisely. That is the mystery."

"Is that so?" He looked puzzled, and irritated too, as if he
was annoyed because this small point had gummed up his
investigation right at the outset. He pulled out the key and

looked at it minutely. He examined the little black men, passing his hand over one and testing its joints. He went over the walls, including the windows.

"Was this open or shut?" he called from the lattice.

"Both just as you see 'em," I told him.

"Damn! I wish the *other* had been open." He went over the corpse last of all, taking a quarter of an hour to scrutinize the clothing and the boots. He then picked up young Saunders' water-sample from the table and came out.

"I'm ready," he said. "Suppose the four of us go down and dangle our legs over the cliff."

Lacking a good perch on the edge of the cliff, we sat on a sizable smooth stone that had been pleasantly warmed by the sun. Veen took out a briar and lit it, and said, "Fire away. Let's have the whole thing over with, the sum total of your faulty memories, unjustified inferences, and baseless conjectures."

It was Jobson's part to lead off, and to do that romancer credit I must say that he made a fine showing. In fifteen minutes he favored Veen with a complete version of his flowery Hearnshaw religion—I don't know what else to call it.

"He was a master among men," Jobson remarked. "He had tales to tell like every other man, but better ones you won't find anywhere. He knew enough of the sea for a lifetime. You couldn't name a port in the five oceans he hadn't seen, and he had such a story to tell of it that you'd think it was his home port. He must 'a' felt terrible here, so cut off from everything—except the women he fancied—everything his life had been, I mean."

Veen exhibited great self-control. "These stories he told," he remarked. "About any place in particular?"

"All places," declared Jobson emphatically. "You couldn't pick a name on the map, sir, without he could give you a yarn about it."

"Yes, yes," soothed Veen. "Yes. It all amounts to this, I suppose. Captain Philip Hearnshaw came here some ten or twelve years ago, and first stopped in the village and then discovered the shanty up here that he later converted into the fo'c's'le, and lived in it. He gave out that he was settling down here after his travels, which for all you *know,* may not have been further than Syracuse or the county jail. He had a small bank account in Newark. He took no one into his confidence, unless it was some of his women. We don't know which, if he did. He had a glib tongue. His voice—"

"Was about like mine," I offered.

"Thanks," Veen responded. "Now that I've summed it all up so far, Jobson, suppose you go on with yesterday. When did you see Captain Hearnshaw last?"

The crestfallen Jobson descended to matters that couldn't be embroidered, and gave account of the Captain's demand for loam and for primroses, and the rest of it.

"I wish I could accuse you gentlemen of being dirty liars," Veen said in the end. "Perhaps that will come later. Now I think it's time to close up for the day. Tomorrow I'll make a search with the object of finding how the parties to the mystery got out of there."

"There were parties, then?" said Jobson.

"Two or three men and a woman, unless I miss my guess," he answered, "and I'm not including you and your young woman of last night."

"I see," I said. "But though I am only a humble onlooker, Mr. Veen, may I offer a suggestion?"

"Certainly," he responded, "if you'll tone down the sarcasm."

"You want to get your two or three men and a woman—not Jobson's girl of the night before—out of the cabin after the Captain's death. So do I—but as I don't see a chance of doing it, why not try to get them out before his death instead? Doesn't it look to you as though he must have been alone when he died, if we're going to keep our senses?"

"Yes, it does look that way, if you leave out one thing," he agreed. "If Hearnshaw had been shot or stabbed or poisoned, or if the gash on the head had finished him, he might have struggled to the door and turned the key and pushed the bolts himself before he collapsed. Only, as far as I can tell at present, he didn't die in any of those ways."

"How did he die, then?"

"Don't think I'm jumping to conclusions," he said. "I say this with reservations, but it looks like drowning to me. I agree with Mr. Saunders that he's been in the lake. And I think, gentlemen, if you're willing to help, that we'll remove the body to Middlehaven. We can use the cot for a stretcher and cover the body with the Captain's blanket."

19

Vivien!

AS A PRECAUTION against marauders and the curiosity-driven, Veen said that he would sleep in the fo'c's'le until the end of the case. He borrowed covers at the hotel and assured Mooney he would sleep in the armchair and be perfectly comfortable.

He asked for some reading matter. "I don't want to think about the problem while I'm falling asleep," he said. Veen looked over Mooney's tattered and torn collection and chose three. One was a Malory's "Morte d'Arthur," and the others were crime stories, "The Mystery of the Freckled Waistband," and "Murder by Compass."

I was present and was moved to comment. "I don't know much about that Arthur book," I said, "but you can tell from the outsides of those thrillers that they're the bunk. Do you actually enjoy them—?"

"I read them by the hundred," he retorted calmly. "All grist to the mill. I may not enjoy every page, but at least I may find ideas in them. How can I tell, Mr. Williamson, that some day an idea from one of these tales may not help me to solve an important case?"

"Has one ever helped you yet?" I asked. "Honest, now?"

"Well, no," he admitted, squirming a little, "not exactly."

"I guess you must like them then."

He had his dinner and went on up to the fo'c's'le.

Next morning he went on with the investigation to find out how the two or three men and a woman had got out of the cabin. He hadn't found out by the time Jobson went up there to notify him that the Coroner had arrived in Middlehaven. I didn't need to ask, when I saw him, if he had made the expected discovery.

Nor did it help the situation when, after a postmortem and an inquest, it was announced to the world that in spite of the gash and in spite of the closed room Captain Hearnshaw had come to his death by drowning. The water in the lungs and that in the sample Saunders had taken were the same.

Detective Veen was supplemented by more officials before his first day in Middlehaven was out, State Police and a
sheriff's deputy. But they were seen no more after the
inquest, and the tall, dark man continued on the ground
alone. But we gathered from the papers that elsewhere
others were pursuing routine parts of the investigation,
looking for the yacht, looking for suspicious characters,
looking for Captain Hearnshaw's past.

From the papers, I also learned of developments in the
big city I had left. The ultimate finding of Mason's body,
barely identifiable, had earned the front page for one day
only. Freddy Brovard had his hour there again as the
doctors certified him fit for the asylum rather than the
electric chair.

Two weeks passed, three, more. Veen remained, sleeping
in the fo'c's'le, probing, prying, puffing his pipe when filled
and drawing at it when empty. Once or twice he called in a
locksmith or other helper. He had been going to "examine
the Captain's papers," but was disconcerted to learn that
Hearnshaw had left no papers—literally none. I sometimes
visited him, prolonging my own stay for a while before
attacking my own problem again. The truth was, I enjoyed
Middlehaven and the broad air of the lake and the broad
land of the countryside, and I was loath to return to the city,
where my own search would have to recommence. I expected no trouble tracing, even back among the years,
anyone with the name of Philadelphia Boston.

Veen kept eating up the vile detective books that
Mooney's provided until he had absorbed the last, and he
was left with nothing to read one night, so he dropped in at
Jobson's in the hope of getting a nibble there. It occurred to
me that the Pat-Dubrosky letters were as good as a book,
though he'd have to provide the end of the story for himself.
It would violate no pledge, and Veen might even have some
helpful suggestion to make, having lived most of his life in
this part of the State. I fished the photostatic copies out of
my case and offered them to him with the remark that they
made a pretty little mystery in themselves and that I was
looking for the treasure primarily, but wanted to find the
woman first.

"Thanks, I'll be glad to have 'em," he said. "Hardly a
night's reading, though."

"Oh, I don't know," I differed.

"I still have Malory up there," he said. "I'm going through the 'Morte d'Arthur' again, and I'll do an extra bit of it when I get through these."

Next day when he was back in the village and returned the letters, I was eager to learn his opinion of them. But he hemmed and hawed.

I felt a vague alarm. "What's wrong?" I asked. "You don't think—this isn't the place after all?"

"It's the place, all right."

"Then what's wrong? It must be the same girl they tell of here."

"Oh, yes, yes," he admitted, but with his finger thoughtfully alongside his nose. "Only—have you ever heard of Marjorie Daw?"

"I seem to have," I said. "But I don't know in what connection."

He smiled. "Mooney has a book named after her," he said. "Thomas Bailey Aldrich wrote it. Look it over. This girl, the writer, seems to me a lot like the young man in the book."

I visited Mooney's bookcase, with a strange, uncomfortable feeling. And when I had read the story from which the book was named, I stood right there for half an hour staring ahead of me, feeling sick and sicker in turn. But then I thought of Dubrosky's one letter. "That was no forgery," I said to myself. "And if it's the real thing, then the whole thing is real. I'll keep my tail up and see what happens."

By this time the Hearnshaw mystery had cast widening circles and taken in the country. As soon as it was evident that this was a real problem, we began to have an invasion, three invasions—tourists, cranks, and reporters. What with these and with the natural inquisitiveness of the village, which increased as the summer residents began to arrive, it was necessary to put up posts and a line to prevent the sightseers and what-not from pressing down the cabin walls.

There were fewer reporters than cranks by a long shot, but there were enough to make me nervous. Half a dozen big female names were on the scene, doing the thing from the sob-sister angle. Since they couldn't get their hooks into any other of the Captain's partners, they picked on Maggie Mooney.

One of the last of the women to appear—though I had more or less expected her all the time—was my little acquaintance from the Women's Press Association, Miss Louisa Matthews Carmody. I happened to see her first and was half in doubt whether to lie low or talk to her again. Of course I was Ex-Warden Peters to her. I didn't make up my mind that day, but I did so quickly the next when I saw her at the bus stop, waiting for Charlie to take her out of town.

"Why, Warden!" she exclaimed, and her brown eyes were really pleasant. "Imagine meeting you here! But perhaps you're getting a story, like the rest of us."

"No, I'm not in the writing game," I said, looking down at her neat hair, sleeked back, for believe it or not, she was carrying her hat as she had in Franklin. It was very delectable hair. "And I have yet to have the pleasure of reading a story of yours."

"Oh, you may yet," she laughed. She drew a cigarette from her silver box and looked inquiringly at me.

"Thanks, I'll have one," I said, and felt for matches.

She handed me a paper with three or four left in it. As I lifted the paper with the flame, shieldingly, my eye caught the words "Gardenier's Hotel—Ask any Traveling Man." I smiled, offered the paper back, but she said she had plenty more.

Then, as she inhaled, she remarked. "I've been up on the cliff and seen that funny little hut thing, and I know all about it."

"Including the answer to the riddle, maybe?" I said.

"Oh, certainly."

I shot her a glance full of suspicion, for I wasn't sure she wasn't serious. She might be a crank too. But her eyes laughed back.

"What's the answer?" I said.

"Well, you can tell your friend the funny detective man if you want to," she said. "He's been reading the 'Morte d'Arthur' up there, I notice. The answer is Vivien!"

The bus drew up and went away with her in it, leaving me half-strangled in a thin blue cloud.

20

Veen's Vertigo—and Mine

"AND IF THAT YOUNG Red Saunders were here," said Veen. "It would be perfect. But since his vacation had a limit, we'll drink his absent health."

We drank his absent health. We drank for this purpose the juices supplied by the Prohibition Bar.

"I asked you to come up the cliff this evening," said the detective, "because I'm going away. Yes," he continued, as Jobson and I both exclaimed, "I'm not permanent here. Mrs. Veen is a patient woman, but I have no intention of trying her patience. I can't pretend I'm doing good here any longer. Also," he added thoughtfully, "I'm getting tired of sleeping in this chair."

Veen rubbed his nose a bit. "This is a desperate measure, gentlemen. I'm about where I was the afternoon we carried the Captain's body down the cliff. Only I'm more certain that the cabin itself conceals the secret. The water that Saunders collected is the same as that in the lungs, both indistinguishable from lake water. That establishes that the Captain was drowned in the lake. That proves an outside hand. Doesn't it, Mr. Williamson?"

"It does to me," I said.

"It does to me," he said.

"And to me," put in Jobson.

"Exactly," said Veen. "You know all this, of course, but I'm clearing the way. I've pulled a great many strings since coming here, but they all come away bringing nothing with them. I've tried to trace the mysterious vessel you saw or thought you saw that night. Not a trace. I wanted to examine the Captain's papers, but he had no papers. Not a paper. He had evidently burned every letter he ever received. Some do. It's canny. I tried to get information as to Hearnshaw's past life from the village. But they're all like you, Jobson. Not a soul, from old Mother Hutchins to Swampy Marsh, knew a damn thing about him—definitely.

"Just reach down that big pad from the shelf, will you, Jobson?" said Veen. "There's a pencil or two handy." The nurseryman, looking mistier and mistier, complied.

"I propose that you keep the minutes," said Veen. "I'll run over the points of the case while you act as secretary, and you, Mr. Williamson, listen. You're my critic. Hold me up if there's the slightest doubt in your mind."

"I see," I said, "I will."

Then commenced an astonishing hour. Rapidly, methodically, exhaustively, Mr. Veen covered every loophole and cranny of the case. He proved the fo'c's'le had been a sealed space by taking it apart section by section. He used a sort of Socratic method, with Jobson as his foil, checking the matter of the door, the windows, the lattice, the walls, the floor, the ceiling, the roof, and the fireplace. Broadening (I recognized his borrowings from detective fiction), he mentioned, only to reject, loosened staples, keys held with pincers, hinges temporarily removed, dummy nail-heads, reputtied panes, movable panels. He bemoaned the fact that the water in Hearnshaw's lungs, and not the blow on the head, had carried him off.

"For then at once the murderer—call him that—can be removed from the fo'c's'le. Think of the multitudinous ways there are of killing a man when he's not in your presence! A poisoned postage stamp to lick—a dagger rigged to fall and skewer him—a poison to vaporize and choke him—a snake to crawl through the ventilator and bite him—"

"Good heavens, sir," cried Jobson, "I never thought there was that much cunning wickedness in the world."

"There isn't; I'm quoting from fiction."

"You don't suppose, sir," offered Jobson tentatively, "that he stuck his head in a pail of water and was drowned that way?"

"No, Jobson, I do not. There would have been the pail to spirit away, you know." After a pause, he added, "My God, what an insane situation! I'm afraid of this place. Sometimes I get dizzy, turning over and over with these facts. I'm afraid I'm going to suffer from vertigo again tonight."

"I don't know, sir, as I'd take it so hard," soothed Jobson. "After all, by and large, does it matter how they got out? What difference will it make in a hundred years?"

The detective dropped into his armchair and consulted with himself before he answered. "As for the hundred years,

I won't be here to tell. But human acts aren't performed on that basis and human minds won't conform either. Perhaps I'm off my balance, but in this case the *method* looms up big, it fills the whole picture. It's the starting point and the ending point, and, by James, we haven't reached it—or any hope of reaching it."

His eyes had been closed. He opened them suddenly and looked full at me. "That's Amen for me," he said. "What does the critic say?"

Both Jobson and Veen suddenly looked at me with a startled interest. What I seemed to them I can't guess, but I too was suffering from vertigo, only of another sort.

"Are you ill, Mr. Williamson?" exclaimed Jobson. "You're fair white at the gills."

"You look as if you'd seen a ghost," said Veen.

"I've seen something," I said unsteadily, my voice hardly sounding my own. "Let me be—let me think."

I buried my head in my hands in a happy confusion, raising it to look about the room in a long scrutiny. Then I jumped up and reached for my hat on the long shelf. "Coming, Jobson?" I asked. "Mr. Veen has closed the case."

"Not so quick," cried the detective. "What's on your mind? Sit down, man. You look ill."

"I wish I could be ill every day," I snapped back. "But I'll stay for a minute, only I'll be Socrates for a change. I've only got a minute."

Veen seemed to regard me with both fear and pity. "Certainly, anything you like," he said smoothly.

I half sat on the table, pointed my hat at him. "What do you do when you have two and two to add up?"

"I make four of them."

"Yes, by thunder! So you do. But suppose somebody gives you two more?"

"Then I make it six."

"But have you?" I cried, and he put his hands on the arms of his chair and partly arose, but I pushed him back. "Remember, Mr. Veen, I told you yesterday about the woman writer I met, and the tip she handed me after she saw you were reading that Arthur book. 'Vivien,' she said. Get that 'Vivien'?"

"Yes, but—"

"You don't pay any attention to crazy tips. No. But you'll soak up all the detective trash you can lay your hands on, and—never mind. When I asked you who this Vivien was, what did you tell me? Why, you said that Vivien was the dame who learned a charm from the old sorcerer Merlin and then locked him up in a hollow tree-trunk with it. I remembered that story from some college course, and you okayed it. Right?"

"Yes, but—"

"No, I'm Socrates now. You're adding up, remember. That's Two. Do you get me? That's Two."

He just looked at me apprehensively.

"Two is what *she* said. Two More is what you yourself said a couple of minutes ago—if you knew the way these mysterious visitors got away after leaving the Captain here, you'd have the whole case in a nutshell. That's Two More, Mr. Veen. Get my idea?"

He nodded, but he lied.

"And the Last Two you got from me! Yes, from me. Two and Two and Two—add 'em up. As sure as death and taxes, Six is the answer. Don't have a headache, Mr. Veen. Pretty soon there won't be a mystery here any more. Now I've got to hoof it. See you later."

I jammed my hat on, grabbed Jobson, and got out.

21

"You, You, You!"—"No, Never!"

THE OUTSIDE AIR SMOTE my forehead cold, but my fever went on. It was an overpowering shock to have the problem of months worked out from nothing to its solution inside of a minute, but above the excitement was a fierce happiness because I had snatched the heart of the mystery right out from under Veen's nose.

With the flabbergasted Jobson beside me I took seven-league strides down the cliff, sometimes laughing, sometimes flinging my arms like Saunders the Red.

We scrambled down into the village in twenty minutes. The Prohibition Bar was less lively than it must have been during the Captain's good reign. I pushed Jobson in ahead and followed him, looking about for Charlie, the frowzy driver of the Middlehaven bus, whom I knew as an institution. He was sitting at a table discussing a glass of beer alone.

I upset his beer for him, grabbed him by the collar, and in spite of his protests, "No, *sir;* no *sir,*" I had him out of the Bar in jig time. He was foggy and I leaned him against the wall. "You ought to pay 'em to ride in that decayed heap of yours, Charlie. But I'm going to pay you to take me up to Newark. How's that?"

"No, *sir.*"

"Ten dollars for the trip," I said.

Charlie all but choked. "Done, *sir,*" he said clearly, without a trace of inebriety. "Have the ol' bus out for you, Mr. Williamson."

It was a mad hour's ride to Newark while Charlie made nothing of the ruts and potholes and I clutched anything clutchable. It was not so very late when we emerged from the dirt and rolled along the concrete main street, to the darkened station.

There was a train-board I couldn't read in the darkness, and I searched my pockets for a match. Eventually I came up with the paper that Miss Carmody had given me, and at the same time my eye caught the sign electrically lit, that showed across the street.

A strange, wild logic possessed me, together with a kind of triumph I had felt only three or four times in my life before. Once was in Flanders when, without reports or any outward sign, I had anticipated an enemy raid and picked the spot where it would come, reasoning—if it was reasoning—just from the situation and the lie of the land. I had placed machine guns in position in time to give them hell. You may call it taking a chance, but it was really taking the only chance—to win. I had made a decision that an onlooker must have called a guess, and it worked.

So now, just as I was scratching a match to read the train-boards—and my eye caught the sign opposite the station: "Gardenier's Hotel—Ask any Traveling Man"—I made a quick move.

I had paid Charlie and he was turning the bus. I leaped in his way as he completed the last arc.

"Hey?" he called, and in answer to a purely imaginary question said, "They's a feller comes along about train time to flag her if you want her."

"Never mind the train," I said. "I'm going to Gardenier's Hotel. Take me there and wait for me. I guess that ten isn't worked out yet."

Inside, I flagged the clerk as he was disappearing toward the back with mop and pail. "Evening," I said, and so did he, adding an inquiry if I was looking for a—

"I'm looking for a woman," I told him. "There's one staying here, isn't there?"

He seemed to think my intentions were very, very bad. "What name?"

"Carmody," I ventured, feeling my heart hop anxiously.

"Yes, she's registered," he admitted, "but she's probably gone to bed."

"Oh, yes? Let me tell you, my lad, she probably hasn't gone to bed. And if she has I'll see her anyhow. Take me up to her."

He saw that I meant to go whether he showed me up or not. He dropped the pail and mop and led the way upstairs. I set down my case and followed. Down the dim corridor on the third floor we went and halted before the door of the room where I had seen the light. I motioned him to run along. Alone, I knocked.

"Who's there?" came her voice, surprised.

"The Warden of Franklin Penitentiary," I answered, "calling to see Miss Philadelphia Boston."

There was a fluttery sound inside, steps across the floor, and the door was flung open. By the yellow electric light in the room to which her back was turned, her face was hardly visible, but I could see that it had lost its demure, rather appealing mouselike look. But now it had a twist of horror in it, and her thin lips seemed to tremble. Her white-streaked hair was loosed and hung over her shoulders, elbow-long. She clutched a gray kimono at her breast.

"What was that name you said?"

I repeated it.

"What do you mean? Why should you give that name to me?"

"Because I know it's yours. Because I've had the biggest hunch of a lifetime. Because, Miss Carmody, if you're Philadelphia Boston, and you are, I have the biggest surprise of a lifetime for you!"

"What do you know about Philadelphia Boston?"

"What do I know about her?" I raised my hands above my head. "I know all about her—you. I know she was the girl, just a kid, that Hearnshaw or whatever he called himself was mad about when he skirmished along this coast twenty years ago. I know they met whenever she could sneak away from home or school, and she called him Dubrosky and he called her Pat. She would have done anything for him. She wanted to jump over the moon. And he wouldn't let her. But he kept on seeing her, doing things for her, showing he was crazy for her too. So in the end—"

She was leaning both hands on the door now, and her head against her hands. Her kimono had fallen away from her breast.

"So in the end she went with him. Or would have gone. Or tried to go. And they were parted in the end. Or no, not at the very end. He was going to die. Perhaps only pretended that he was going to. Perhaps that's what he wanted her to believe. And later—" I said what had come to me of a sudden—"later after the Boston house had been destroyed when the woods were burned, he came back. He found Middlehaven grown up, but no one knew him. So here he lived. And then you came to him the other night."

She had not changed her position. I put my hand on her shoulder. "You had looked for him for a long time, hadn't you? You had searched every prison in the East. And then you learned that he was here. And it was you that came and took him from the cabin and brought him back and left him there and went away again."

She raised her head. She gathered her gown about her again. "How do you know all this—that you *say* you know?"

"Two and Two and Two!" I cried. "The mystery you left behind you with the Captain's body was no mystery at all if you knew that everything depended on the way you went out, and if you had read the letters, and if you knew what Vivien meant! That last you gave me yourself, remember."

"Letters! What letters!"

"Yours, Miss Pat, that Dubrosky kept so long and then lost somewhere. Your own letters gave me the hunch."

"You mean—you have—the letters!"

"Sure I have—copies anyhow. I've had 'em since—no, that's something else again. Can't tell you about that."

"The letters!" she murmured. "The letters!" It looked for a while as if nothing could shake her from that.

Suddenly she shook her head. "You are clever, aren't you?" She put out a wan little hand and touched me. "Clever Mr. Warden Peters." Her voice rose. "No, Mr. Clever Warden, that was not Philadelphia Boston. And I am not Philadelphia Boston."

Her words had a convincing sound. I saw all my logic smashed to flinders. "What—what do you mean?"

"There's been no Philadelphia Boston—no, not for years and years."

I retorted desperately, "I don't believe you. It's you, you, you—"

"No, never!" She upped with her chin, and her voice shook with laughter. "You don't believe me? Who should know, you or I?"

"Well, for God's sake explain yourself then."

"Not tonight, not tonight. But I don't mind that you should know, Mr. nice clever Warden. You will think more of me, perhaps. And it is good, I have found, to have even an acquaintance think well of you. Will you meet me tomorrow night, at the ruin where the Boston house used to be?"

"The ruin—?"

"There. Come after nine o'clock. I will bring the woman who did these things, and she will tell you."

"You will bring—?"

She retreated into the room, took the handle of the door. "Tomorrow night."

"But wait!" I cried. "You haven't heard the biggest wallop of all. The treasure—Dubrosky's treasure—"

"No, no, not tonight!" Head down, arm extended, she dismissed me. The door closed.

So I rode back to Middlehaven with Charlie.

22

The Other Woman

SO I WENT TO THE RUIN of the big house in the woods by night. A thin, cold mist straggled in the trees, but the moon was high, and it was not dark there. I went on foot along the deserted road, and passed by the broken gateposts and along the weed-grown drive toward the standing wall, and toward the lake of which I caught glimpses through the northern barrier of the woods.

I had walked around the house two or three times, and had turned off into a desolate garden-walk, when I saw a solitary figure approaching me from the lower end of the garden. I presumed that there was an old entry there, perhaps leading from the water.

My first glimpse of the figure was a shadowed one, but in another moment it emerged from beneath an elm. On it came, the slightly overplump figure, suggesting stays, the dress all ribbon and flounce and feather, a dozen queer shades in the frosted moonlight. Her little feet had the queer pointed walk I remembered. She came on, all white shoulders, her cloak flung back, and wild reddish hair standing out about her head, with a jewel in it. She came very close to me, and I saw the make-up on her face, varying tints of red and blue and even a glimmer of green at the ends of her eyes, whose lashes, greased and slicked, gave the eyes themselves a starry expression. She stood right there in front of tongue-tied me, and her lips, crimson an inch wide, bent and mocked me.

"Mr. Peters, you recognize me, eh? Soh!" It was the Countess de Sieffert herself speaking!

"Yes—Countess," I said with quickening breath.

"And you recognize me too, Mr. Warden Peters?" asked the voice of Miss Carmody from the painted lips.

"Yes—you—too."

The lips smiled. "I am the other woman, you see. Do you understand? This painted person, this made-up crea-ture—is the one I spoke of last night. Doesn't my wisp of

Bohemian accent sound natural? I lived with it so long that it *is* almost natural to me now. Soh!"

I was furiously backtracking over my long course, picking up clues, patching pieces together, finding answers. In a flash, I had accepted the fact that the woman who had visited Franklin Prison, the woman who had waited with me in Gray Mason's room, and the woman at the heart of this mystery, were one and the same. I cursed my eyes, for not detecting resemblances under differences—then damned my wits, which were really responsible. I had not thought. The Countess de Sieffert—only there was none—

She had changed in an instant. She shook her head vehemently and frowned. I had a moment's thought that this was like an angry child. Her features contracted and her small fists grew hard.

"You understand everything now, Mr. Warden Peters? You know why I have come to meet you this way? You know what I meant when I told you last night that it was not Philadelphia Boston who visited the cabin the night the Captain died? Not a shadow of Philadelphia Boston left."

I looked at her wonderingly. "Aren't you going to tell me about it? Last night—"

"I sha'n't be that way again. Last night you stormed me, took me by surprise. Tonight will be different. You won't hear my voice falter, I promise you. Suppose we walk for a little while," she suggested. "The mist is cold. There is not often mist here, except in the spring, like this." She had drawn her cloak up over her shoulders, and I put my hand through her arm and shortened my steps to hers.

She said, "You have read the letters—later you must tell me how you got them."

"I've read some of them, but I have only the copies."

"I am not ashamed to have you read them. You know that?"

"There is nothing in them to be ashamed of, Patricia," I said.

"No, they were real Philadelphia Boston. She had nothing to be ashamed of. Perhaps I was a little—restless. So was my mother, you know. I said a lot about her, didn't I? She ran away with someone, too—but that was later of course. My father was a nostrum seller. You gathered that. Unfortunately, his mother was still living when I was born, and she had belonged to one of the quite mad sects that were so thick in this part of the country, and she would have me named Philadelphia. Father was still just enough impressed with the humbug to allow her to do it. But afterward, though he never told grandmother about it, he told me how sorry he was for the name, and that I should make up one for myself and take it when she wasn't here to raise a fuss. She was supposed to have money, you see, but it turned out that she had lost it in speculation. And father's business petered out, and he had never been much of a saver, giving lots away to queer little religions that grandmother told him needed to be fostered. But I wasn't going to talk about that. . . . There was a man . . ."

"Yes," I said, "the man Dubrosky."

"The man Dubrosky," she agreed gravely. "I don't think I want to tell you his real name. It isn't Hearnshaw, of course. At first he had been received in our home, and he had played with me. He seemed another father, a far-traveled one with hundreds of wonderful tales that fascinated me. But I was hardly in my teens before I told myself that I was in love, and I was. His stories and my reading had aided in making me precocious, and then one year I was kept out of school because I was absorbing things too fast there. That year—with Dubrosky! I loved him. I made no secret of it to him, either. How could I when every instinct in me and every restraint my foolish mother tried to put on me made me feel that I was his!"

We turned at the end of the path. The weeds had made the most of their long supremacy, and the damp from the growing things was smeared on her gown and wrap.

"Well, you know all that. You told me last night—how those words of yours brought it all back, Mr. Warden Peters!" She touched her forehead with her fingers. "There are memories here that had slept until you awakened them last night. How he tried to prevent me! How he reasoned with me, thinking that I would listen to reason! In the end, of course, though he left this place, intending never to return, I followed him, and when he had gone so far that it would have been impossible for him to bring me back without scandal, I joined him. That was abroad. So I won."

She paused again, for there must have been thronging memories for her in those three words, and I blundered in a question.

"He wasn't what you'd call a marrying man?"

"He had a wife already," she said, "but they never saw each other." She turned on me a little fiercely. "Mr. Warden Peters, I want you to know that Dubrosky was—a gentleman, a decent gentleman. But I was too much for him, that was all. It was a wonderful time we had together, but good things never last. Mother and father had first tried to have me detained or arrested, and when burning up the cables did no good they came after me abroad. But quite independently of anything they did, Dubrosky left me. He went away, and left a note and money, and told me to go home. It would be bad enough now, he said—he always spoke plainly—but if we went on together it couldn't end except in the worst kind of misery for me.

"Do you know what we did then? Mother and father decided that since scandal had raised its head at home by now, it would be a good idea to stay abroad for a while. We made a European tour, in fact three European tours, one each year, though our home was in England, in Sussex. I never heard anything directly from Dubrosky during all that time. Once or twice there were bits of news that might be about him, and I took the chance of sending him a forwarding address, where I thought it might reach him. But I never heard from him, and I often wondered if he heard anything of me.

"But no sooner had we come home than everything happened at once, at least so quickly that it seems almost instantaneous now. Mother ran away with a—creature. That's all I can call him. Poor father didn't live long after that, and I was alone in the house, except for grandmother, who was the only relative I had left.

"Grandmother survived father only a few months, and the week after she died I left this house for the last time. I went in search of Dubrosky. I never found him."

In spite of her promise, she broke off, and we once more turned at the ragged end of the long path in silence. I felt her give a sort of shake or shudder. She spoke again as we came closer to the house.

"I'm not going to tell you much about the next ten years in Europe, Mr. Warden Peters. I met—men, I suppose you'd say. Among them was Jean de Sieffert; he's still living. There had once been a title, but it is only a family name. I used it, and Countess improved it. I drifted in a hectic sort of life, the capitals, resorts, casinos, and the rest. I was hardly twenty, and life was calling. I wanted Dubrosky more than anything else in the world, yet all that I ever heard of him was that he or someone like him—the name was not the same—had died of fever somewhere in Russia. Only the fact that I had met someone I used to love very much, and who loved me, brought me up out of the—out of the hell I was in."

"Mrs. Mason," I said.

"Yes, Harriet Boyd. I had known her at school, and we found each other over there, both unhappy. She had married in Europe several years before, and I knew her husband, knew him from once when I was rather a little girl, and he came here once or twice as our guest."

"Clever Julian," I said.

"You have all the names right, Mr. Warden Peters. He had once been a criminal, but when Harriet Boyd met him he was strolling about Europe very much the gentleman with a clever, taking manner. She had just had a wretched affair with someone else, and Julian Sand, or Mason as he called himself, was there to catch her on the rebound. When I met her, she was making the most of appearances, though she had despised her husband for years."

The moon had slid over our shoulders while we walked and she talked. Now she seemed to notice the compound shadow that we cast.

"It's growing late, isn't it?" she said. "I've said too much about these earlier things, and yet I wanted to. It relieves me of so much that I have not told to anyone else. It is good to have someone, not too close to me, a friend, an unintimate friend, to tell my secrets to." She looked up at me and smiled, and tucked her hand a little further into my arm.

"I must get on to the night that has caused so much excitement and speculation here. But you don't know, do you, how it was that I came to this shore again?"

"No, Patricia. That's one of my chief mysteries."

"It was that night you broke in at Mason's—after you left. I found what I had been searching for, and it brought me here."

"That doesn't mean anything to me."

"I had been in Gray Mason's house for many weeks before you came that night, and I had made earlier visits. As the Countess de Sieffert, of course. I had made Harriet realize that he must not know who I had been. For Clever Julian had known a secret of my mother's, which was why she feared him and did not want him to come when father invited him. And later I too had a reason why I didn't want Gray Mason to know that I was Philadelphia Boston, for fear he would be on guard against me. Do you know why he might be on guard?"

I had a glimpse of it, but I said for her to tell it.

"Because he had my letters, the letters that you in some mysterious way have read. Once during an earlier visit I had seen the corner of one lying on that desk of his. He was showing me a picture—he was always proud of his photography, which he liked almost as well as checkers. But my eye caught the corner of the letter, over which he had thrown some other paper for concealment. I went faint, for I not only knew that in all probability Dubrosky was alive, but that Gray Mason was blackmailing him. At least I thought it was blackmail then, not knowing his methods. And suddenly I knew that I would never be at rest until I found Dubrosky again."

"Just a moment, just a moment. Give me time to think," I said. "I've got to rearrange part of my mind. Mason blackmailing Dubrosky, or at least threatening him? But when you came to Franklin, Patricia, you were doing just one thing, no matter what else you pretended. You were looking for Dubrosky."

"That was clutching at straws, Mr. Warden Peters. For when I did one day speak of Dubrosky, under his true name, as someone I had known, Mason would say nothing of him directly, but hinted that he had done enough to get him into prison, and keep him there the rest of his natural life. I simply made up my mind to visit every prison in the East, and either find the man, or satisfy myself that Mason was lying. That's how I made your acquaintance." She made a pressure of emphasis on my arm.

"It was a long way round."

"Yes, but what else could I do? I made more than one attempt to get the letters, but they were apparently gone. At that time I didn't know anything of hiding places in Mason's room. Later, when I had spied and watched, I saw that I might need aid. And the night that Madeleine Brovard died, I watched you, Mr. Warden Peters, because I had recognized you.

"I had been wondering about them, the Brovards. I wondered if Mason and they were, perhaps, partners, and I tried to find out—"

"Quite so, Patricia, I saw you through a keyhole. But the pictures—what about the pictures?" I demanded. "Didn't anyone find them? I expected you to get them sure."

"Yes, never fear, I picked up the packet that Mason dropped as he struggled in your arms. I got it, and besides, I removed from the room one or two peculiar implements that your friend brought—or the matter might not have been kept private after all. I did those things immediately and I hid the implements and looked quickly through the pictures as soon as I reached my room. There were some rather frightful scenes among them, but nothing that meant anything for me. So when the house was quiet I went back to Mason's room again."

"For the invisible letters!" I exclaimed.

"For the letters and the heater."

"You were looking for a letter to Dubrosky."

"And I found it! That was a moment! It told everything in a minute. It made my other life live again—almost. That was because it told me that—Dubrosky was still living. And it told me where he was!"

"It was a menacing letter, like those others?" I asked, as she seemed to fall brooding.

"Yes! Oh, how I laughed, deep down inside myself, when I read those threats of Gray Mason's. He had written to Dubrosky quite recently, though when he had met Dubrosky it must have been years before, and he had stolen the letters then. But Dubrosky did not know the thief. That was clear from Mason's words. On the basis of what he read in the letters Mason made up his accusations; out of the letters he created a monstrous charge, that what had been between Dubrosky and me so long ago had been wicked, had been criminal. Mason treated Dubrosky quite differently from his other victims. Evidently he did not believe he had succeeded in rousing him to a pitch of fear, and now he actually threatened exposure and prosecution, and he quoted letters in such a garbled way that they might have been awkward to explain in court. But it was all ridiculous—you see that, don't you? Unless Mason could produce me and I perjured myself, there could be no case. And he did not know who I was."

I said Yes, she was right.

"He didn't know who I was, though I was under his nose all the time. No wonder I laughed. Mason was actually threatening to send the letters to the District Attorney. He said they were in their envelope, and he would post them within ten days—"

"One moment, Patricia. About when was the date of Mason's letter? Can you remember? Think hard."

"Oh, yes, it was some date in January a year ago—a year and a half ago, you see."

I gave a satisfied grunt. "Thanks."

"I thought only of finding Dubrosky again, and of the amazing fact that he was here, in Middlehaven! I hid Mason's letters away—they're still mostly in my trunks in New York, along with your friend's implements—and I told Harriet only that I was returning to this part of the State. I was eager—terribly eager to see Dubrosky again. And yet, right then and there, I thought my dream wouldn't come true. Can you guess why?"

"Maybe because Dubrosky would have changed."

"Yes. . . . He would have changed." We went a little in silence, then he said, "Do you suppose we might sit down for a little while? I'm warm again now."

She pointed to an old garden seat for two, an ironwork relic, half in the shadow of one of the unscathed beeches. I scoured it vigorously with a few handfuls of grass and spread a handkerchief for her to sit on.

"Thank you." She took her place. "I have bored you, Mr. Warden Peters, by all this talk which has so little to do with you. No—I mean it. I have only just come to what has caused all the trouble and excitement here in Middlehaven, the part that stirred you to so great excitement last evening and brought you here tonight.

"I have only just come to the fringe of the mystery, as I suppose you call—"

"Mystery be damned! I know enough to tell you the solution of the 'mystery,' at least in outline. What really caught me and brought me here was this Other Woman business."

A voice broke in behind us, accompanied by a shuffling in the grass, "But I should be very glad to hear the explanation that Mr. Williamson—or is it Peters?—disdains."

We twisted sharply; at first the man was indistinguishable in the shadow, but his figure dislocated itself from the darkness. It was the black-suited, black-hatted Veen, with the dark face.

"Good evening," he said calmly.

"Good evening!" said Patricia.

"Veen!" I exclaimed. "How in the devil did you get here!"

"By addition," he answered in a self-satisfied tone. "From you I learned to add to Six. Charlie the busman gave me information today that brought the total to Eight, and to-night, being in the Bar and seeing you slip out carefully, I added Two more and made Ten. Like a problem in Poe, you know. I rather enjoyed it. I simply followed you here, Mr. Williamson, or is it Peters?"

"Either will do," I answered. "D'you mean to say that you've been here all this while, listening—"

"I crave the lady's pardon, but if she will let me hear the explanation in her own words—" He made it a question by breaking off. "I unfortunately have to know, you know."

Patricia's voice was not displeased. "Yes, Mr. Detective, but there is so much that you have missed, things that my friend and I have spoken of while we were walking up and down."

Veen bowed. "I was about to say that I will ask the gentleman to supply any additional details that may be necessary. You will give him permission, will you not?"

"Why, certainly."

He stood before us with arms folded. "Then I shall not interrupt you, Madam. Please proceed."

23

"But Good Things Never Last"

FIRST OF ALL, MR. DETECTIVE," she resumed, "you must promise that you won't annoy the people who have helped me. I mean the men who brought me here tonight, and who took me to Dubrosky's, twice. They have done no harm, except lying."

"To me, eh? When I was trying to check on the boat Mr. Peters saw offshore that night?"

"Yes, I asked them not to tell. They are men who used to work for us at Two-mile, and they have done this for me. I don't want them to get into trouble for nothing. I don't want you to try to trace the whereabouts of the yacht or find the men. I couldn't prevent you right now if you walked down to the shore and arrested the man there with the dinghy. But have I your promise?"

"Don't put me on my honor," begged Veen. "You have no idea how uncomfortable you make me, Madam. Suppose we just leave the subject."

"Thank you!" she said.

The detective bowed slightly, and his pipe kept on puffing.

"Mr. Peters, may I have a cigarette? Thank you."

Patricia smoked right down to the butt before she spoke again.

"Well, then," she said, "I came to the Lake some time ago. Perhaps I put up at Rochester or Sodus Bay or Oswego—you aren't going to inquire about that, Mr. Veen. I had to go where I could find the men. And the first evening I sailed to Rowell's Point at sunset, and rowed ashore and walked up the point of rock, and found no one at the cabin. I had intended my visit for a surprise, but when I found the cabin empty I left a message under the door, saying that I would return the next night."

"There used to be primroses, didn't there?" I asked.

"Yes, there used to be."

"That was it, then," I said. "Early youth and sadness. They fitted all right."

"Dubrosky told me how he got those flowers that next morning. It was like him, you know, an exaggerating thing to do. And it was unlucky, too, horribly unlucky."

"What do you mean?"

"You'll see. I'll tell you everything as Dubrosky did it after getting my note that evening. From what he told me the next night and what I gathered in the village and up at the cabin later, I've put it all together. He was tremendously surprised, and he lay awake nearly all the night, remembering and planning. He was glad that I had come. I couldn't have told that; I couldn't have known. Because he was glad, he thought of the flowers. There had been many kinds he planted in the big earth-boxes up at the doll's house in the old time, pansies and snowdrops and sweet peas, but I had liked the primroses best. It was because he wanted something there to be just as it had been before that he bought the flowers from Mr. Jobson, and made those long trips up the cliff. For a man of his age, it was a hard task. It took him all day. Then evening came, and it looked like rain, and he commenced to wait there in the doll's—but here I am, taking it for granted that you both know that the cabin had been the doll's house that Dubrosky had built for me long ago."

We assured her that we had guessed.

"Then while Dubrosky was waiting for a sight of my boat, he saw someone coming up the cliff from the village, and he remembered that he was supposed to have another guest that evening—that girl Maggie. So he simply locked the door on the inside and made a horrible face at her when she came around to look in the window. He succeeded in scaring her away. But afterward he wondered if she wouldn't fetch someone and come back.

"He saw your lantern, Mr. Peters, as the three of you came up the cliff, and this time he walked out, leaving the cabin open. While you were looking over the place he was in the underbrush, counting the seconds until you'd clear out. By the time you had gone, the lights of the yacht were showing off the point. There's an easy landing for a small boat there. The two men who had rowed me in remained with the boat and I went on up the cliff alone.

"The cabin was lighted now. There was a big lamp over the small door at one side, throwing enough light to make a path for me from the edge of the cliff. I came nearer and had just caught a glimpse of the flower-boxes with the primroses, which I knew hadn't been there the evening before—when the whole front of the house came apart, the halves of the wall opening outward, and Dubrosky was there, pushing them wide, to his arms' width! He looked like Samson. I realized that the feature of the building that I had thought so wonderful when I was a little girl had been retained or restored. That is, like smaller dolls' houses that you buy in stores, this one was made so that by opening it you could see the whole interior at once. When it was closed, the weather-strips concealed the break perfectly. He had often told me that he made it so snug and had concealed the hinges in the corners so carefully that unless the building was taken to pieces board by board the secret would not be found. When he had come back he had cut a smaller door in the left hand side of the wall, but that had made no difference in the folding halves of the wall themselves."

"It is like that," said Veen. "We did some taking apart this afternoon."

"I was afraid so. Now I wish I had told you before you tore the house to pieces. Is it completely—demolished?"

"Very slightly," assured Veen.

"I'm glad. But there's hardly any mystery left. As I came up, the walls widened and came to rest with a shock. Then he laughed and came toward me. . . . I went inside the cabin. He closed the walls in, just leaving them open a crack. Inside the cabin we sat and talked . . . for a long time . . . I thought he was nervous. . ."

There were little pauses here and there in her story now. They didn't come as gaps of emotion, but more as moments of thought.

"I looked at him, and at first I thought how little changed he was, except that his beard had once been short and trimmed and now was wild and ragged. But then I looked at his eyes and saw little twitchings of his bearded face, and I wondered if he was well. I asked him straight if he felt right, and he laughed and said Yes, certainly, but he'd been having interruptions all evening long and he was still jumpy from the fear that someone else might bob up, or the same ones again. Then I suggested that he should come with me on board the yacht, and he instantly agreed.

"We went out together through the wall, so to speak, and Dubrosky didn't bother to make the halves of the wall fast. He laughed and said it would give anyone who came some more to think about. We walked along together. . . . It was quite a horrible thing that happened there as we picked our way down Rowell's Point. Dubrosky had been walking beside me, and suddenly he wasn't there any more. I had heard a scuffling beneath me, than a splash, before I realized that he had gone over the edge. It must have been his heart. . . . The exertion of getting the earth and the flowers, opening the wall of the doll's house, even the climb down the cliff. . . . And so it was that he fell and was stunned and couldn't help himself in the water. He was drowned almost before my eyes."

This time the pause was a little longer.

"I screamed, of course, and the men came hurrying from the boat. Then the moon went out, and it began to rain. I held both lanterns and they went down the rocks to get him. It took quite a long time though the water was shallow. . . . It was quite shallow water he was in. But the blow on the head had stunned him. They tried to revive him. The rain was terrible. It was cold, too. I said that in the cabin it would be warmer, and it was not so far away.

"There had been a fire inside the cabin when I came in. It was still burning well and they pushed the bed aside and laid Dubrosky down on the floor and went on trying to save him. I don't know how long it was, perhaps an hour, more likely two, before we gave it up. I had taken my turn with the others, and all of us were losing our strength and courage. . . . Suddenly I couldn't stand it any longer. I had seen it was no use, but I had let the men go on.

"When we had hurriedly gone outside and had gone a little way from the cabin, I insisted on returning and closing the halves of the walls. The men, of course, had no idea how to shut them fast, and I had to do it myself. Dubrosky had shown me again just a few hours before. I am so low in stature that I had to be lifted in order to reach the catch, concealed—you know how, Mr. Detective?"

Veen's pipe had gone out long ago. He hadn't relit it, but he still caressed it. He nodded somberly. "Neatly done," he commented. "One long rod reaching down from top to bottom."

"Well, that's all, you see," said Patricia. "When I was on the ground again, we went away. The smaller regular door, which Dubrosky had built in later, had been locked all this while. But I didn't know this, of course, and I couldn't have considered the consequences if I had. I simply didn't dream that the finding of Dubrosky's body would make such an apparently unsolvable mystery. For these weeks I have been hovering in the background, more or less uncertain what I ought to do. I assume that you recognize me through this bedizenry, Mr. Detective?"

"I have been noting resemblances," he acquiesced, "Vivien."

She rose briskly. "Then I must go. That moon had hardly begun when I came. There is nothing else you want of me?"

"No, Madam." Veen bowed.

I spoke to Veen, rather huskily. "Wait for me here, will you? I must see the Countess—Pat—this lady alone for a minute."

We moved toward the shore, left him standing in the path. I was almost raving with excitement. There were the pictures, for one thing. I hate loose ends, and if there was still a chance to get hold of Raffy's picture, I wanted it, wanted it damnably. But towering above that there was the untouched topic of the treasure. As we walked to the end of the path, I burned with the desire to tell her the great secret, the thing which I knew and she did not.

"Patricia," I said, "there's something else, something you didn't speak of, haven't thought of, perhaps, for years."

I thought I read a hint of alarm in her moonlit face. "The treasure," I said. "You've forgotten about Dubrosky's treasure."

I waited a long while for a response. "Why do you think so, Mr. Peters?"

I groped for the meaning of this. It sounded strange.

"I don't understand you, Patricia. You don't understand me either. I found out something I've got to tell you. That treasure—those trinkets—glass—whatever you thought them—weren't worthless as you thought. They were real jewels—worth a fortune!"

She looked down at her hands, her fingers twining and twisting.

"I know," she said. "I knew it long ago."

"You knew! But you couldn't have known! His letter never reached you. It was never sent."

"His letter?" I saw only her eyes looking out of her face, staring up at mine.

"Dubrosky's letter—he wrote it when he was sick—kept it when he got well, I guess. I told you that the treasure—but you say you know already."

"I said I knew long ago." She smiled bitterly. "You are going to have everything, aren't you? Even what I would have liked to keep back. If I wanted you to say to yourself romantically, 'Through it all, she was true to him!' or something like that—no chance now. Philadelphia Boston would have been true, I think."

She sighed. "But good things never last. I suppose Philadelphia Boston came to an end that day she visited the treasure cache again."

"Wind, earth, and water," I quoted.

"You know that too, do you?" She shrugged. "Why am I trying to tell you anything at all? You keep ahead of me. But you didn't know—I took—the treasure."

A world of comprehension came over me. I echoed, "Took it!"

"Yes? Do you know what 'Wind, earth, and water' meant?"

"Not exactly. But I might guess."

"At the end of Rowell's Point, where the bottom is never exposed unless the wind is off the shore—there in the mud alongside a big rock Dubrosky and I had buried the treasure—with ceremony. And when I had come back from Europe—and him—I revisited the place one day. The ice piles up there terribly in winter, but the rock and box were still there. I found the old rotting box, and pried it open. Then I saw those gewgaws with more than a child's eyes. I knew that the glittering things weren't glass. I knew I had found an actual treasure, and I took it. I took it and I used it, Mr. Warden Peters—at first to find Dubrosky then afterward when finding Dubrosky had no more place in my mind. But from the moment I reached down my hands and rifled the treasure—there was no more Philadelphia Boston. God knows, that's what I've been trying to tell you tonight."

"He said he wanted you to use it—to live gloriously. He said there was enough to enable you to live ten lifetimes, gloriously."

Her lips curved bitterly. "Did he? He hardly knew what he was saying, I think. I've had a bit of living gloriously, and I know what it means—just one life of it. Look at me; isn't that enough? Good night, Mr. Warden Peters. Thank you for your patience."

She held out her hand again, and now I saw that it contained the packet that Gray Mason had taken from the picture frame. "They are all there," she said. "Take what belongs to you, and then, if you heed my advice, you will burn the rest. I wish I had never seen them. I'm not squeamish, but whatever Gray Mason touched is—defiled."

"Thank you, Patricia. If there is anything I can ever do—"

"Can't you guess?"

I stood like a nincompoop for half a minute before it dawned on me. "Your letters!" I said.

"And his. Can you?"

"Yes, Patricia. Where do I send them?"

"To Harriet Boyd, to Mrs. Mason. Thank you, Mr. Peters. I wish Philadelphia Boston could thank you, but she's—gone. For *me* it's been nice to know you and see you these three or four times. But good things never last. Do they? . . ."

I hesitated. "I'm not so sure." I found that she was gone. But if warmth, fragrance, tenderness had formed Philadelphia Boston, it was not true to say that there was no more of her.

24

Raffy Strikes

I TORE THEM into tiny pieces, and scattered them over the landscape from Syracuse to Cortland on the Lackawanna line. When the bits of the last one, except the two I was saving, disappeared into the fields, I felt better. They had been a burden to me ever since the evening before when I had examined them in my room.

There was nothing monotonous about the photographs. Among the non-obscene was one which showed a wagon-load of hay being hoisted into the upper story of a barn. Another was an automobile license-plate shot close enough to show that there had been tampering with two of the numbers. Another showed a man's nickeled shaving kit laid out on top of a dresser, his initials on several of the pieces contrasting with those embroidered on the cover of the dresser. There was a portrait of a little lad holding a Scotch terrier tight against his chest and laughing at something the camera didn't catch. Of them all, I think I have oftenest speculated what was the story behind the picture.

I had no difficulty choosing what Raffy wanted. One print showed his face and another his legs, both unmistakable. The legs had it for importance, as between the feet lay a head, a head rather like Raffy's with the same smooth insolence of cheek and jaw. But this head had two little punctures in it before the left ear, and one of them had bled, the blood running down to the eyebrows, where it had curdled.

A little blood had also run onto Raffy's spats. The other picture showed Raffy with his gun held at his waist, staring down at something that lay between his feet. There was no sign of anyone else and nothing in the background that showed where they were taken.

The photographs placed a somewhat different in-terpretation on the death of Raffy's brother from that current in the underworld and adopted by the police, namely that a hop-fiend had shot Jake Sabati the night that Raffy had come into power. A certain indistinctness and spottiness in the prints suggested that the camera had looked through glass, and I was suddenly enlightened as to the circumstances under which Gray Mason had left half his coat hanging on a shutter-pin and the other half in the gutter. Raffy's crime and the finding of the Pat and Dubrosky letters had occurred on the same night.

The immediate future was planned. I had taken the Lackawanna because it went through northern New Jersey. I intended to get off at Dover and hire a car out to Aldrich's that night. After my report I had no doubt that I'd get the real letters from him, and I could send them to the writer next morning.

Then there would be Raffy. I hadn't made up my mind what line to take with him. Whatever it was, I wasn't likely to expose my ace in the hole, the pictures that were now tucked in the inner pocket of my vest. Whatever the method, I was going to conclude a peace with him that would get me rid of him and his crowd. For unless I took measures, I saw myself pestered, interfered with and perhaps disabled or rubbed out, as long as I remained near New York.

It was a warm day, the first of June, and I dozed off in the observation car. When I awoke suddenly late in the afternoon, I found that the train was standing at the Dover station, and I leaped to my feet to make a dash for my baggage and the platform. But I sank back again with my head spinning. Opposite me, over a magazine, was the ugly mug of Peru. His eyes were significant. I glanced at the pocket of his coat. It bulged.

The train pulled out from the station. We didn't say anything.

My head settled, and I looked about the car. The seat on my left was empty, but on the other side of me, toward the observation door, a big, frog-like man was sitting sideways, looking at me. His pocket bulged too. He had been at Raffy's the night I had walked in behind Mr. Dockety. A third man, enveloped in tobacco-haze, was sitting at the entrance to the narrow passage toward the front platform. I knew he was one of Peru's party.

I wondered what would happen if I made a move of any sort. On board a moving train, what would they dare? While

I wondered we came to Summit, and the train slowed down. Peru got up, and so did the pair I had associated with him. Peru, his eyes on me, jerked his chin just perceptibly, as much as to say, "Come on." The big frog-like chap was right behind me. I went out with the three and the big man picked up my suitcase where it stood beside my chair.

We walked out of the station, the third man leading the way, Peru and I next, and the big man bringing up the rear. There was an old Packard parked around the corner. We got in.

I wasn't stunned, but thinking did me no good. I couldn't figure how Raffy's finger men had trailed me. But I sweated when I thought of the two pictures in my vest. If there was any way of disposing of them with these three thugs at my elbow, I didn't know it.

It took more than three hours to get from Summit to Fifty-seventh Street, Manhattan, via the Holland Tunnel. But we didn't stop there. Peru leaned forward and growled to the driver, who drove on to a drug store several blocks further uptown. We waited while Peru went in and 'phoned. Then we drove up the Washington Heights and on beyond the Harlem River, crossing the Bronx toward the north-east.

My mouth was exceedingly dry. I asked, "What do you guys think you're doing?" This was almost the only remark I had made.

Peru gave a thick laugh.

Somewhere in the Woodlawn district Peru telephoned again, after which the driver turned back toward Manhattan and hit it up. I had a glimmer of hope that we might be pinched for going fifty or so, but the speed cops must have been arresting college boys just then.

It must have been in the neighborhood of eleven o'clock when we drew up in front of the house on Fifty-seventh Street and they hustled me across the pavement and through the door, which the doorkeep held open. They crowded me up the stairs to the top floor, past a dark second story. The tables weren't running tonight, it seemed. Everything nice and quiet for my reception.

I found myself in the front room of the top floor, where I hadn't been before. It was Raffy's office, brightly lit, and Raffy himself faced me across a big flat-top desk. Still a fashion-plate, rose in his buttonhole, opal pin in his tie, he was thinner, I thought, than when I saw him last, certainly paler. For me he had the pleasant welcoming look of a dog for a rabbit. He lifted his eyes to the three who were standing beyond me in a row.

"Have you frisked him?"

"Nope," said Peru.

"Get busy." Expert hands slapped me up and down.

"Nuttin' on him," said Peru.

"Go through his pockets, you dumb!" snarled the Guk, and while I faced him eye to eye Peru and the greasy one stripped me clean of everything I carried, including the envelope with the pictures in my inner vest pocket. When the pile was complete on the desk, Raffy picked up each thing, scrutinized it, chucked it down. He came to the envelope last, and opened it and saw its contents. His face took on a horrible grimace of hatred; if I hadn't seen the change I'd never have recognized that twisted mask for his countenance. He tore the prints twice across and made a little heap of the parts on the mahogany surface of the desk. With a match he ignited them. Silently we watched them burn.

When they had turned to ashes, he crushed them and brushed them away, leaving a scar on the desk, and ordered the three men: "Beat it. Wait for the buzzer."

They got out. The man carrying my suitcase tossed it down beside the desk.

"So you knew Holborn," cried Raffy. "You and Holborn was pals, and he sent you to get me! That's the low-down on you, Fultz, ain't it? You and your pictures!"

I just blinked, but I was surprised enough to flop back against the wall. It was enough to find that Raffy the Guk and Holborn were connected in some way, but to discover that Raffy suspected me on his account was more—plenty more.

"What you talking about?" I said. "Who's been spieling you?"

"No back talk, Fultz," he snapped. "Peru was in your room down on Avenue A, boy. He saw everything."

"Talk sense," I retorted. "What the hell do I care about Peru?"

"Peru can read, see? He knew Holborn's writing, all right, all right."

It was true enough that among the letters were notes in
Holborn's hand. Raffy had deduced from that fact. Even
now the notes were in my suitcase. I thought of telling him
so in order that he might see that he had been barking up
an empty tree, but he jabbered at me.

"That was my woman Holborn went with in Jersey, see?
You know that? You know what happened to him, doncha?
Yeah, you know, all right."

I had a memory of Holborn saying, "I've been framed . . .
but it doesn't matter." So now I knew the truth was in him.
But I was learning too much at once. I couldn't digest it. I
wanted time.

"You scragged the woman, eh?" I said. "And then framed
him for it. That what you mean?"

"What the hell else do you think I mean? I wanted you to
know, Fultz. What happened to him is going to happen to
you."

I snarled back at him. "You flat-skull, d'you think you can
get away with a thing like that twice? Not with me, you
can't."

He was quite pleasant about it. "Listen, you. You bumped
off Wally Stemholzer, didn't you? You're goin' to the
hot-seat for it."

"Like this guy Holborn, framed, eh?" I said. "I don't know
what you're talking about, you mutt—do you?"

He shook his head at me, showing his teeth in an ugly
smile. "Think you're God damn clever, don't you?"

"What is this, a game?" I asked.

"Keep on talking, boy," he said. "I'm wise."

"You're cuckoo," I said. "What's happened to Stemholzer,
anyhow? Hasn't he been around?"

Suddenly Raffy stood up. His smooth hands were
clenched on the edge of the desk. His eyes narrowed to slits
of hate, and his voice changed to a wild beast's snarl. He
spoke with his lips drawn away from his teeth.

"Listen, you! I'm a guy gets what he wants, see! I want
you rubbed out, get me? You damn double-crosser, come in
here from Milwaukee, did you? Milwaukee across the river.
You knew Holborn, you snitch. Goin' to play the nose in my
racket, wasn't you? Goin' to get those pictures for me, and
then cross me up, wasn't you? Yeah! You knew Holborn all
right, didn't you?"

"What's it to you?"

"Sure, I knew it, you tripe." Only he didn't say "tripe." "Friend of Holborn, nosin' around here. Goin' to get the pictures for me—after Mason croaked, wasn't you? Swell chance."

He had never believed in my good intentions, then, that morning after the housebreaking.

"You and Stemholzer," he boiled. "A couple of lousy noses, both playin' around with my girl. I'd of bumped you off long ago, you—"

"You're cock-eyed," I said. "You ape, are you standing there trying to tell me that I wanted your girl? How dumb some dopes can be!"

But he ignored my remarks. "I got Stemholzer, and you're framed to take the rap. Yeah, you can't beat Raffy. By God, Fultz, the cops have been lookin' for you, and my guys have been tailin' the cops. You can't beat Raffy, you know that? Get me, boy? It's goin' to stick."

I could have laughed in his face if the pictures had still been in my vest pocket.

"You tell me one thing," said Raffy. "Where—?" He flicked his head quickly to one side as the door behind me opened suddenly and Peru's voice sounded worried.

"Say, boss—"

"Get the hell out of here," growled the Guk. "I'll give you the buzzer when I want you."

"But, boss, the door—"

"Downstairs, and stay downstairs till I want you!" blazed Raffy and lifted his fist threateningly. He was white with rage. He advanced on Peru, shouted down his pro-tests—Peru never did get across his message—and next to booted him out.

"Of all the damn fools I ever saw," I said, "you win the rubber gun, you do. What do I know about Stemholzer? I don't even know he's dead."

He leaned back on his heels, hands at his belt, looking at me with a look that was half malevolent, half sarcastic. "Nerve you got, Fultz," he said. "You're goin' to need it when I get the boys up here workin' on you. You're goin' to need nerve when they take pieces outa your arm, boy."

The 'phone rang. He glanced at it, hesitated, and then grabbed the receiver.

"Yeah?" He had hardly time to say the word when his voice seemed to be snatched away. He listened, and a new rage took possession of him; he breathed hard through his open jaws. He listened for a long time, perhaps twenty seconds, before he found his voice again. "Yeah? yeah? The God damned—"

He didn't finish, dropped the receiver, not on its hook, and reached for the buzzer button at the corner of the desk.

At any time since the 'phone had rung I might have hopped on him and tried my strength as a last resource, only for the thing that had kept me hesitant throughout, that button eighteen inches from his elbow. I could have prevented the use of his gun, wherever it was, but not that button. Now I had lost my chance, my last chance, as I saw his fist plank down on it.

There was a lull while we faced each other. Raffy had forgotten me. The 'phone call had been potent. I waited. Any minute, any second, might produce anything.

There was no sound from outside the door, from the stairs. Raffy punched the button again.

The door opened behind me. I didn't turn to look, until I saw the expression on Raffy's face. Then I wheeled and spun back almost against the wall. Through the door, closing it after coming through, had stalked the appalling ghost of Wally Stemholzer, bearded with bunchy whiskers, bandage at the neck, suit hanging on him as if it clothed a skeleton. He never took in my presence, at all, perhaps never saw me. But he held a gun in his hand (he wore a yellow kid glove on it) and with his gun he pointed Raffy to his big black leather chair. Raffy, as if hypnotized, obeyed.

"Sit down," said the apparition, "and keep your hands out of your pockets." The voice was hoarse and croaky. Seeing Raffy's eyes wander toward the buzzer button again, Stemholzer said, "That's no good. Your doorkeep put it on the fritz. He's left. You know what it cost me? Five grand. You should have paid the old boy better. Five grand would have saved your life, Raffy. You're too damn Scotch. I'm the other way. Generous, I am."

Stemholzer made three unsteady steps across the room and stood on the other side of the desk from the Guk.

"I'm going on a summer cruise, Raffy," he said. His voice had fallen to a raucous whisper. "They say it's the best thing for me, after what you did to me down at the studio. Dead? No—just not quite. I've bought passage on a boat, a sailer, without any wireless or radio or anything, and I'm on my way to it now. I just stopped in on my way."

He paused. I looked from him to the Guk. Raffy sat intensely quiet, but his eyes wandered, wandered.

"Oh, yes, I was going to tell you, Josephine's coming too. She's my nurse; isn't that a good one? She was sort of coy for a while, but when she'd looked over the boat she forgot all about that. She likes her comforts, Josephine. Virtuous, but mercenary. She's been sour on you for a long time, did you know that? I didn't tell her anything about coming here, though. She won't know, not ever. We'll be out of touch with the world, you know. Won't read about you in the papers. Well, I guess that's about all. You're for it, Raffy."

I saw Stemholzer shifting his gun a little, screwing his eye, taking deliberate aim. I heard Raffy give a kind of squeal, and when I turned my eyes to him he had swung forward, reaching toward a drawer of the desk. He had his hand on the drawer, bent over, when Stemholzer fired one shot. Raffy slumped down dead, with his head under the desk.

Stemholzer dropped the gun on the floor and went out, closing the door behind him. I didn't hear his footsteps in the hall.

I moved over to Raffy, turned his face up, saw the hole the bullet had drilled in his forehead, went around the desk, picked up the gun, opened the door a little way, and listened. There wasn't a sound anywhere and I figured that if Peru and the others hadn't appeared by this time, they hadn't heard the shot. The door had been closed. They were still waiting somewhere below for the buzzer.

I took one quick look around Raffy's desk, collected my things lying there, jerked open the drawers, to see if there might be any data about me anywhere, anything, for instance, connecting me with Holborn. There were almost no papers there at all, as I had expected, for racketeers don't leave documentary evidence around. Within five minutes of the shooting I was carefully making my way downstairs through the darkness, Stemholzer's gun in my hand.

I figured that the two flights between me and the door might still be my Waterloo. Peru wasn't the kind to keep on waiting, even if he had been practically kicked out.

Just at the head of the lower flight I paused and listened, still in the dark. I had heard someone coming up, someone who had stopped when I had. I heard another slight movement.

"Who's that?" I whispered.

For answer a flashlight snapped on in my face, blinding me. I sensed a hand groping for me. My finger, pressing the trigger of Stemholzer's gun, pressed it still further. There was a crash and a reverberation, and everything fell away. The flashlight landed on the floor, pointing toward the head of the man I had just shot: Jack Carson.

This was what Raffy had cursed about when he got word over the wire, another visit of the police after all. This was what had delayed Peru and the other pair from delivering me here earlier in the evening and what had kept the game from running on the second floor: fear of a raid. Someone had been doublecrossed that evening, all right.

They were surging about me now, half a dozen of them.

"Is he dead?" I asked. I was cool enough.

The one who had been examining Carson, looked up and said, "Naw. Send for the ambulance."

"Send down to the morgue, too," I said. "There's an honest-to-God dead one upstairs."

~   ~   ~   ~   ~

The lieutenant at the desk didn't smile.

"Where did you get that gun?" he said.

"It's Stemholzer's gun." I said.

"Who is this Stemholzer?"

"Carson knew him. He was the fellow who was there—the one that shot Raffy."

Still the lieutenant didn't smile. He didn't speak.

"He was there, I tell you," I said.

The lieutenant laughed coarsely. "So was Julius Caesar," he said.

25

The Last Chapter

THAT LAST LANE, and the last turning.

Even inside these walls where the ripples on the world's surface fade, Gray Mason's bombshell full of secrets has had its effect. Bursting on New York in a summer of depression and dullness it has kept the news alive ever since. Of course, the tabloid that received the sealed envelope from the vaults of the trust company did not admit its indebtedness to a source it didn't know itself. Oh, no, it was the industry of the reporters that had unearthed these carloads of slime. Give them credit.

We read the papers here. I have tried to guess how many of the scandals revealed and old crimes resurrected and solved were due to Mason's information and photos. Among those which were not included in the packet were Raffy's pair. Not that they would have helped my cause. Shooting a murderer is just as heinous as doing in a vestryman. But I know at least two suicides have resulted from the secrets, and one man has come to join us here in the death house. A prominent Pennsylvania mayor is out of a job, and another has found one, on a stone-pile. I can't count the divorces. All things that seem to make little difference to me, but tremendously important, I suppose, to the people themselves. Yet I wonder sometimes, what does it all matter?

What does it all mean? My own case, considered impartially, is no more—

~   ~   ~   ~   ~

Now it is December. Only a year and three months since the little brown woman came into my office at Franklin, yet it seems a lifetime ago. It all has happened since then, and it all will end so soon.

I've had plenty of time to think as well as write. I believe now I know why Holborn, my friend and not a murderer, decided to send for me the night he went out. He had tried

to be bigger than a man, but he couldn't resist one final
effort to repay a debt of evil. In sending me out on the trail,
where he expected I might meet Raffy, there was a shadow
of a chance—for revenge. Or, was it only a dead man's jest?
Did he think he'd enjoy our play, somewhere looking on?

He had jostled against Raffy, had fallen for Raffy's current
mistress, and had paid the price. How resigned he was, how
unconcerned in Franklin! Genuinely unconcerned. Except
for the gesture just before his death, an automatic action,
the movement of a particle when a vacuum sucks it in. Now
I have fallen foul of Raffy in another way, and I'm following
Holborn where he went from Franklin. It's curious, but I feel
as Holborn did, indifferent. Yes, my case was fought to the
last ditch, and appealed, and the Governor has been prayed
to in my behalf, but in spite of all, I'm content with the
inevitable. I don't rave. I don't curse my luck, or anyone,
not even Raffy the Guk.

Thinking of Raffy, as I have so much these days, a saying
I've always doubted comes into my head, the one about
there being some good in everyone. In the heart of Raffy
the Guk was there ever anything but selfishness and cruelty,
anything but what was foul and rotten? I can't find it, if
there was. And yet it's really for him that both Holborn and
I go to the chair.

That's Destiny (apologies to Ludwig) for you. But I'm not
sore at Raffy, or at my luck, either. I might have had a flock
of witnesses to bring me off, but in the end there was not
one. Six months have gone by, and there's no word of
Stemholzer from any passing ship or foreign port. That's
easy enough to understand, but without the man himself—and I believe he'd come back if he knew my trouble—there's not a shred of evidence that he ever walked up
and down the stairs in Fifty-seventh Street. I was the only
one who saw him in the house. No one can be found who
saw him before or after. The doorman who decamped (his
five grand were gone in two weeks and he was picked up in
Hoboken nine parts d.t.) had never laid his eyes on the
party who had sent him a thousand and promised four more,
and paid it. Peru and his crowd, listening in on Raffy's
phone, had skipped out before the police reached the front
entrance. The gun, which bore my fingerprints alone, had
been stripped of all identifying marks. It was untraceable.
So was the driver, if there was one, who had brought

Stemholzer to Raffy's house and taken him away.

Raffy had burned the pictures; they would have been a help. I was laughed at by every one but the judge when I testified that Raffy had cracked off his brother.

There was, in fact, no backing whatsoever for my own story of that evening, and the fact that I had tried to shoot my way out of the house when the police were in possession was a clincher against me. It shouldn't have been, but it was.

So Raffy was right. He's framed me for somebody's murder—his own! But it's just as binding.

I think that Stemholzer would come back if he knew my trouble. But I doubt if he had heard the New York news where he is, or wants to, cruising about somewhere in the lazy southern seas. Or perhaps he cruises no longer. Drowned men tell no tales, and hear none.

There it is. I examine my case closely and conclude that I've had beastly luck. But what of it? Others have worse luck than I. Teddy Brovard, for instance. I don't envy him. The way I figure it, what a man does never depends on himself at all. You have to get the breaks, and even with the breaks you don't get there unless you're a certain kind of a man. And being that kind of a man is a break too. Being what I was and coming up against things as I did, here I am in the Sing Sing death house waiting my turn.

But I have the biggest break because I happen to be the kind that can laugh it off. What would the best of life be if you couldn't laugh it off? And how much worse is the worst, if you can?

~ ~ ~ ~ ~

This morning I had a visitor. It wasn't until he had taken off his hat that I recognized Aldrich through the screen.

"I'm a fool," he said—although a guard stood nearby, hearing every word—"but I wanted to see you bad. So I've come. That was a tough break, the Governor turning thumbs down."

"Oh, I don't know. What could you expect? A gangster like me!"

"Philosophical guy, you are." He shifted his feet. "I thought I'd come—"

"I'm glad you have," I said. "It saves me writing you a

note."

"Oh, yes? No hard feelings, Peters?"

"None whatever. I went in with my eyes open, didn't I? And if you didn't pay the damn good lawyer who defended me, who did?"

"Yes, I know. But perhaps we don't do things with our eyes open, not as much as we think we do."

"What do you mean?"

He winked at me. A guard can't hear a wink.

"What do you mean?" I repeated.

He winked again. "Always keep your eyes open, Peters," he said. "It's what I call the great rule of life. The other thing may mean death."

"I think I get you," I said.

"That's good. What were you going to write me about?"

"The letters. You don't want them now. Still got them?"

"Yes."

"Will you send them to Mrs. Gray Mason? She'll see they reach the proper party."

"Sure I will."

"Thanks, Aldrich."

"Well, I guess that's all, Warden. Good Luck." He went out. Good luck!

~   ~   ~   ~   ~

Fifty minutes to go.

In the cell, half an hour after Aldrich left, I found a gun. I haven't seen it yet, but I've felt it in the canvas cover of what serves me for a pillow. A gun! I don't know how it got there.

But I know how it may be used. "Always keep your eyes open, Warden." Will there be a break in the death house to-night? If there is, I'll be ready for it.

What are my chances? Not hopeless, certainly. Twice before men have smashed their way out of the window of death in Sing Sing prison. Why not I?

Does the Warden know? Has someone squeaked? Is the Warden waiting for my first move, ready to nip the play in the bud?

No more time to write. Not here, certainly. Perhaps not ever. It all depends—does the Warden know?

THE END

RAMBLE HOUSE's

HARRY STEPHEN KEELER WEBWORK MYSTERIES

(RH) indicates the title is available ONLY in the RAMBLE HOUSE edition

The Ace of Spades Murder
The Affair of the Bottled Deuce (RH)
The Amazing Web
The Barking Clock
Behind That Mask
The Book with the Orange Leaves
The Bottle with the Green Wax Seal
The Box from Japan
The Case of the Canny Killer
The Case of the Crazy Corpse (RH)
The Case of the Flying Hands (RH)
The Case of the Ivory Arrow
The Case of the Jeweled Ragpicker
The Case of the Lavender Gripsack
The Case of the Mysterious Moll
The Case of the 16 Beans
The Case of the Transparent Nude (RH)
The Case of the Transposed Legs
The Case of the Two-Headed Idiot (RH)
The Case of the Two Strange Ladies
The Circus Stealers (RH)
Cleopatra's Tears
A Copy of Beowulf (RH)
The Crimson Cube (RH)
The Face of the Man From Saturn
Find the Clock
The Five Silver Buddhas
The 4th King
The Gallows Waits, My Lord! (RH)
The Green Jade Hand
Finger! Finger!
Hangman's Nights (RH)
I, Chameleon (RH)
I Killed Lincoln at 10:13! (RH)
The Iron Ring
The Man Who Changed His Skin (RH)
The Man with the Crimson Box
The Man with the Magic Eardrums
The Man with the Wooden Spectacles
The Marceau Case
The Matilda Hunter Murder
The Monocled Monster
The Murder of London Lew
The Murdered Mathematician
The Mysterious Card (RH)
The Mysterious Ivory Ball of Wong Shing Li (RH)
The Mystery of the Fiddling Cracksman
The Peacock Fan
The Photo of Lady X (RH)
The Portrait of Jirjohn Cobb

Report on Vanessa Hewstone (RH)
Riddle of the Travelling Skull
Riddle of the Wooden Parrakeet (RH)
The Scarlet Mummy (RH)
The Search for X-Y-Z
The Sharkskin Book
Sing Sing Nights
The Six From Nowhere (RH)
The Skull of the Waltzing Clown
The Spectacles of Mr. Cagliostro
Stand By—London Calling!
The Steeltown Strangler
The Stolen Gravestone (RH)
Strange Journey (RH)
The Strange Will
The Straw Hat Murders (RH)
The Street of 1000 Eyes (RH)
Thieves' Nights
Three Novellos (RH)
The Tiger Snake
The Trap (RH)
Vagabond Nights (Defrauded Yeggman)
Vagabond Nights 2 (10 Hours)
The Vanishing Gold Truck
The Voice of the Seven Sparrows
The Washington Square Enigma
When Thief Meets Thief
The White Circle (RH)
The Wonderful Scheme of Mr. Christopher Thorne
X. Jones—of Scotland Yard
Y. Cheung, Business Detective

Keeler Related Works

A To Izzard: A Harry Stephen Keeler Companion by Fender Tucker — Articles and stories about Harry, by Harry, and in his style. Included is a compleat Keeler bibliography.

Wild About Harry: Reviews of Keeler Novels — Edited by Richard Polt & Fender Tucker — 22 reviews of works by Harry Stephen Keeler from *Keeler News*. A perfect introduction to the author.

The Keeler Keyhole Collection: Annotated newsletter rants from Harry Stephen Keeler, edited by Francis M. Nevins

Fakealoo — Pastiches of the style of Harry Stephen Keeler by selected demented members of the HSK Society.

RAMBLE HOUSE
Fender Tucker, Prop.
www.ramblehouse.com   fender@ramblehouse.com
318-455-6847   443 Gladstone Blvd.   Shreveport LA 71104

RAMBLE HOUSE's OTHER LOONS

Slammer Days — Two full-length prison memoirs: *Men into Beasts* (1952) by George Sylvester Viereck and *Home Away From Home* (1962) by Jack Woodford

The Organ Reader — A huge compilation of just about everything published in the 1971-1972 radical bay-area newspaper, THE ORGAN.

Dr. Odin — Douglas Newton's 1933 potboiler comes back to life.

The Chinese Jar Mystery — Murder in the manor by John Stephen Strange, 1934

The Julius Caesar Murder Case — A classic 1935 re-telling of the assassination by Wallace Irwin

The Contested Earth and Other SF Stories — A never-before published space opera and seven short stories by Jim Harmon.

Freaks and Fantasies — Eerie tales by Tod Robbins, collaborator of Tod Browning on the film FREAKS.

Vixen Scandal — Two sleaze masterpieces from the 60s by Jim Harmon: *Vixen Hollow* and *Celluloid Scandal.*

Maniac Siren — Two more sleaze marvels by Jim Harmon: *The Man Who Made Maniacs* and *Silent Siren*

West Texas War and Other Western Stories — by Gary Lovisi

Marblehead: A Novel of H.P. Lovecraft — A long-lost masterpiece from Richard A. Lupoff. Published for the first time!

The Secret Adventures of Sherlock Holmes — Three Sherlockian pastiches by the Brooklyn author/publisher, Gary Lovisi.

The Universal Holmes — Richard A. Lupoff's 2007 collection of five Holmesian pastiches and a recipe for giant rat stew.

Tales of the Macabre and Ordinary — Modern twisted horror by Chris Mikul, author of the *Bizarrism* series.

The Gold Star Line — Seaboard adventure from L.T. Reade and Robert Eustace.

The Werewolf vs the Vampire Woman — Hard to believe ultraviolence by either Arthur M. Scarm or Arthur M. Scram.

Black Hogan Strikes Again — Australia's Peter Renwick pens a tale of the outback.

Four Joel Townsley Rogers Novels — By the author of *The Red Right Hand: Once In a Red Moon, Lady With the Dice, The Stopped Clock, Never Leave My Bed*

Killing Time — New collection of short novels by Joel Townsley Rogers

Night of Horror — A short story collection of Joel Townsley Rogers

Twenty Norman Berrow Novels — *The Bishop's Sword, Ghost House, Don't Go Out After Dark, Claws of the Cougar, The Smokers of Hashish, The Secret Dancer, Don't Jump Mr. Boland!, The Footprints of Satan, Fingers for Ransom, The Three Tiers of Fantasy, The Spaniard's Thumb, The Eleventh Plague, Words Have Wings, One Thrilling Night, The Lady's in Danger, It Howls at Night, The Terror in the Fog, Oil Under the Window, Murder in the Melody, The Singing Room*

The N. R. De Mexico Novels — Robert Bragg presents *Marijuana Girl, Madman on a Drum, Private Chauffeur* in one volume.

Two Hake Talbot Novels — *Rim of the Pit, The Hangman's Handyman.* Classic locked room mysteries.

Two Alexander Laing Novels — *The Motives of Nicholas Holtz* and *Dr. Scarlett,* stories of medical mayhem and intrigue from the 30s.

Two Wade Wright Novels (and counting) — *Echo of Fear* and *Death At Nostalgia Street,* with more to come!

Three Rupert Penny Novels — *Policeman's Holiday, Policeman's Evidence* and *Sealed Room Murder,* classic impossible mysteries.

Five Jack Mann Novels — Strange murder in the English countryside. *Gees' First Case, Nightmare Farm, Grey Shapes, The Ninth Life, The Glass Too Many.*

Four Max Afford Novels — *Owl of Darkness, Death's Mannikins, Blood on His Hands* and *The Dead Are Blind* by One of Australia's finest novelists.

Five Joseph Shallit Novels — *The Case of the Billion Dollar Body, Lady Don't Die on My Doorstep, Kiss the Killer, Yell Bloody Murder, Take Your Last Look.* One of America's best 50's authors.

The Best of 10-Story Book — edited by Chris Mikul, over 35 stories from the literary magazine Harry Stephen Keeler edited.

The Anthony Boucher Chronicles — edited by Francis M. Nevins
Book reviews by Anthony Boucher written for the *San Francisco Chronicle,* 1942 – 1947. Essential and fascinating reading.

A Young Man's Heart — A forgotten early classic by Cornell Woolrich

Muddled Mind: Complete Works of Ed Wood, Jr. — David Hayes and Hayden Davis deconstruct the life and works of a mad genius.

My First Time: The One Experience You Never Forget — Michael Birchwood — 64 true first-person narratives of how they lost it.

The Incredible Adventures of Rowland Hern — Rousing 1928 impossible crimes by Nicholas Olde.

Don Diablo: Book of a Lost Film — Two-volume treatment of a western by Paul Landres, with diagrams. Intro by Francis M. Nevins.

The Charlie Chaplin Murder Mystery — Movie hijinks by Wes D. Gehring

The Koky Comics — A collection of all of the 1978-1981 Sunday and daily comic strips by Richard O'Brien and Mort Gerberg, in two volumes.

Gamefinger — Incredible 1966 sado-sleaze from Clyde Allison (William Knoles).

Dime Novels: Ramble House's 10-Cent Books — *Knife in the Dark* by Robert Leslie Bellem, *Hot Lead* and *Song of Death* by Ed Earl Repp, *A Hashish House in New York* by H.H. Kane, and five more.

Stakeout on Millennium Drive — Indianapolis Noir — Ian Woollen.

Dope Tales #1 — Two dope-riddled classics; *Dope Runners* by Gerald Grantham and *Death Takes the Joystick* by Phillip Condé.

Dope Tales #2 — Two more narco-classics; *The Invisible Hand* by Rex Dark and *The Smokers of Hashish* by Norman Berrow.

Dope Tales #3 — Two enchanting novels of opium by the master, Sax Rohmer. *Dope* and *The Yellow Claw.*

Tenebrae — Ernest G. Henham's 1898 horror tale brought back.

The Singular Problem of the Stygian House-Boat — Two classic tales by John Kendrick Bangs about the denizens of Hades.

The One After Snelling — Kickass modern noir from Richard O'Brien.

The Sign of the Scorpion — 1935 Edmund Snell tale of oriental evil.

The House of the Vampire — 1907 thriller by George S. Viereck.

An Angel in the Street — Modern hardboiled noir by Peter Genovese.

The Devil's Mistress — Scottish gothic tale by J. W. Brodie-Innes.

The Lord of Terror — 1925 mystery with master-criminal, Fantômas.

The Lady of the Terraces — 1925 adventure by E. Charles Vivian.

My Deadly Angel — 1955 Cold War drama by John Chelton.

Prose Bowl — Futuristic satire — Bill Pronzini & Barry N. Malzberg .

Satan's Den Exposed — True crime in TorC New Mexico — Award-winning journalism by the Desert Journal.

The Amorous Intrigues & Adventures of Aaron Burr — by Anonymous — Hot historical action.

I Stole $16,000,000 — True story by cracksman Herbert E. Wilson.

The Black Dark Murders — Vintage 50s college murder yarn by Milt Ozaki, writing as Robert O. Saber.

Sex Slave — Potboiler of lust in the days of Cleopatra — Dion Leclerq.

You'll Die Laughing — Bruce Elliott's 1945 novel of murder at a practical joker's English countryside manor.

The Private Journal & Diary of John H. Surratt — The memoirs of the man who conspired to assassinate President Lincoln.

Dead Man Talks Too Much — Hollywood boozer by Weed Dickenson

Red Light — History of legal prostitution in Shreveport Louisiana by Eric Brock. Includes wonderful photos of the houses and the ladies.

Gadsby — A lipogram (a novel without the letter E). Ernest Vincent Wright's last work, published in 1939 right before his death.

A Snark Selection — Lewis Carroll's *The Hunting of the Snark* with two Snarkian chapters by Harry Stephen Keeler — Illustrated by Gavin L. O'Keefe.

Ripped from the Headlines! — The Jack the Ripper story as told in the newspaper articles in the *New York* and *London Times.*

Geronimo — S. M. Barrett's 1905 autobiography of a noble American.

The Compleat Calhoon — All of Fender Tucker's works: Includes *The Totah Trilogy, Weed, Women and Song* and *Tales from the Tower,* plus a CD of all of his songs.

The Naked Trocar with **The Best Revenge** — Two misdemeanors by Fender Tucker from 2007

www.ingramcontent.com/pod-product-compliance
Lightning Source LLC
Chambersburg PA
CBHW030332020726
47493CB00004B/1246